WHITE HOLIDAY

WHITE HOLIDAY

by

VIOLA BAYLEY

COLLINS
LONDON AND GLASGOW

First Edition 1953

PRINTED AND MADE IN GREAT BRITAIN BY
WM. COLLINS SONS AND CO. LTD.
LONDON AND GLASGOW

CONTENTS

CHAPTER ONE

THE BLUE MOON

"Rose, what the dickens do I call this?"

"M'm?" Rosemund's dark head was bent over a letter. "Call what?"

"This what-not from Aunt Lucy."

Will gingerly held up a small cloth object between his thumb and finger.

Rosamund signed her name with a sweep of triumph, laid down her pen, then folded her arms and considered the object from all angles.

"Well," she announced thoughtfully. "It might be a pen-wiper. No, more likely something to polish your shoes with. It *could*, of course, be a queer sort of book-marker. Oh dear, I'm getting writer's cramp! How many letters have you done? I've done six and I've got five more."

The two sat opposite each other at the old school-room table. It was Boxing Day, and the task of thank-you letters was for the moment slightly obscuring the joy of the Christmas presents themselves.

Will was seized with sudden inspiration.

"I know!" he cried. "I'll just put 'Thank you most awfully for your most useful present.' How's that for resource?"

There was silence while both heads again bent over the old table.

7

It was a pleasant room, the school-room, hardly altered since nursery days, when Rosamund had learnt to walk with the aid of its friendly chair-legs. It was still the children's own retreat, although Rosamund had just left school, and Will's long lankiness had little in common with the stout cherub whose photograph hung over the mantelpiece. At intervals Mrs. Burnaby suggested new curtains or an improvement in the way of a fresh chair-cover, or even a total migration from the top landing to the back study, but all such suggestions were indignantly repudiated. So the school-room remained as it was, with its low ceiling and dormer windows that looked over the neighbours' gardens. Where better could one watch old Mr. Farman taking his afternoon nap in the garden of No. 3, his newspaper over his eyes; where better speculate on the young and noisy family opposite, rioting behind their uncurtained windows? It would have surprised the inhabitants of Beck Street considerably had they known the fantastic doings that Rosamund's imagination had credited them with over the years.

At last Will rose. He was a tall boy of fifteen, whose round cheerful face still looked mildly surprised at the distance it found itself from his feet. He stretched himself, yawned, and ran a toe thoughtfully along the patch of Indian ink on the hearthrug.

"Rose! Is Dad terribly hard up?"

The sudden question brought Rosamund's pen to a stop. She looked up quickly at her brother.

"I don't think so," she said after a moment. "Not to worry about, I mean. Of course we all know what Daddy's like over his fees. If someone comes and says ' Dear Mr. Burnaby, I'd give the world to have you to be my counsel but I haven't two brass farthings to rub together, Daddy just won't charge any fees at all. Bless his heart, it's lovely to be called the poor man's champion, but poor Mummy has a bit of a thin time balancing the budget. I think the Vandermeyer case was the only one that really paid last summer."

"The American woman with that poisonous son Loo-is?" Will chuckled at the memory. "Wonder if we shall ever see them again?"

"I shouldn't think so. D'you remember how she came and almost wept on Daddy's bosom after he'd won her case? And then she said all that about asking us to stay next time they were on the Continong. Oh well, out of sight, out of mind. That sort of thing just doesn't happen, not even once in a blue moon. What's the time? Everybody's out. Let's go and make some hot-buttered toast in the kitchen. After that I shall have to iron my frock for the party."

"The Matthews' party! Good lord, I'd forgotten about that," groaned Will. "Dancing, bah! Think of doing the hoky-poky with Dolly Matthews. Does that girl ever stop giggling?"

"It won't be too bad," said Rosamund soothingly. "I only hope to goodness nobody treads on my blue net again. It's got frightfully torn. May Matthews said she supposed I was keeping my new frock for to-night. You should have seen her face when I said I only had one."

Will caught the wistful tone in her voice and turned to survey her.

"I wouldn't care what old May says," he remarked loyally. "Just jolly well snap your fingers at their new frocks. You can beat 'em into cocked hats anyway."

Rosamund smiled gratefully at Will, then turned to the old mirror on the wall. The grey eyes with their fringe of dark lashes stared gravely back from the small oval face. It was a charming and expressive little face that mirrored—sometimes with embarrassing clearness—the light and shadow of her thoughts.

She gave herself a little impatient shake, as though to rid herself of the visions of exquisite frocks that would insist on floating through her mind.

"Toast ahoy!" she cried gaily as she flung open the school-room door and clattered down the back stairs.

The kitchen was warm and comforting. It was Mrs. Elkin's day out and therefore Mrs. Fez-Fusby was the sole occupant thereof. She had taken up a strategic position on the arm-chair near the stove. She was a lady of great dignity if somewhat obscure parentage, and even maintained a Victorian and distant relationship between herself and the offspring that from time to time staggered and tumbled about the kitchen. That Mrs. Fez-Fusby was an unaristocratic cat even the children couldn't deny, but even Mrs.

Elkin agreed that "there was a somethink about that dratted cat—acts like she might be the Queen of Sheba." The origin of her name had been lost in the mists of antiquity. Perhaps it had something to do with the black ruff inherited from some far-off Persian ancestor.

At Rosamund's entrance, Mrs. Fez-Fusby opened one eye. There was slight inquiry in the glance, for Mrs. Elkin being out, the usual saucer of milk had not been forthcoming.

"Miaow?" said Mrs. Fez-Fusby.

"Fuz-Buzz, darling, we'd forgotten you!" Rosamund was all penitence. "My poor sweetie-pie! Was it a hungry pussum?"

She was the only person in the household who dared take the liberty to talk baby language to Mrs. Fez-Fusby. It was while the lady in question had graciously accepted a saucer of bread and milk, that there came the sound of the front door opening, followed by voices in the hall.

A moment later Mrs. Burnaby hurried into the kitchen.

"Hallo, darlings!" she cried. "I'm simply frozen. Daddy and I had to go to poor old Mrs. Jennings' funeral."

Rosamund pulled her mother down into the lately vacated arm-chair. Mrs. Jennings had been a cantankerous old neighbour who had bullied her friends and relations unmercifully, and Rosamund's wrathful face showed that she considered being buried on this icy day the crowning act of Mrs. Jennings' selfishness.

"I wonder where she is now," mused Will.

"Heaven, I suppose. She was always so particular about knowing the right people."

"Will, darling, you really mustn't!" remonstrated Mrs. Burnaby. "Oh dear, how nice it is to be home! Hot-buttered toast? And tea all ready? How gorgeous. Daddy has just gone up to change. We'd better eat in here. I don't expect any one remembered to make up the drawing-room fire."

"Sorry, Mum, I clean forgot," said Will. "We were knocking off our thank-you's in the school-room. Oh gosh! Look at that bit! Burnt to a cinder. That comes of talking to the man at the wheel. Any news from the outside world?"

Mrs. Burnaby considered a moment.

"No, nothing special," she said. "I met Mrs. Matthews in the Square and she said how much they were looking forward to seeing you to-night. Rose, do bring down your dress. I want to see if we can make another fold to hide that tear down the back."

Rosamund started for the door, only to collide with her father, who was on the point of opening it. Diverted from her purpose, she pulled him into the room and displayed Will's very creditable pile of toast.

"Excellent. Just what I need."

Mr. Burnaby smiled aimiably at his family, his keen legal face softening as it always did in the bosom of his home.

"I stayed a moment to listen to the weather forecast," he remarked. "They predict snow. I shouldn't be at all surprised."

"Mrs. Elkin says the snow has got into her bones already," said Rosamund. "It always seems to arrive in her bones long before it gets anywhere else. It must be awfully uncomfortable. Worse than a depression off Iceland."

Mr. Burnaby leaned back from the table to search in the pockets of his coat.

"I've got an article on the migration of birds somewhere here," he said. "It'll interest you, Will—fascinating subject. Dear me, I think I must have left it in my greatcoat. You'll find it hanging in . . . By Jove! This had completely slipped my memory."

He drew an envelope out of his pocket and handed it to his wife.

"For you, my dear," he announced. "I hope nothing urgent. It came to the office I'm ashamed to say three or four days ago. I seem to know the handwriting though I cannot place it."

Mrs. Burnaby tore open the envelope, disclosing several sheets covered in a large sprawling writing. She glanced at the signature.

"Mrs. Vandermeyer!" she cried. "I wonder what she wants? She is writing from some hotel in Cannes."

She glanced swiftly through the first page and then gave an exclamation of surprise.

"David, this is most extraordinary! Do listen! Do you remember that she said something about asking the children for a holiday? I never thought she really meant it, but apparently she did."

Rosamund gave a wild leap across the hearthrug and was kneeling by her mother's chair. Will sat

back on his haunches, his face red with excitement
and toasting.

"Mum! Where? Quick!" begged Rosamund.

Mrs. Burnaby turned again to the first page.

"' Dear Mrs. Burnaby,' she read, ' don't say
you've quite forgotten me for I shall never forget
you and that marvellous man your husband. I
tell every one in the States that our barristers are
just nowhere with David Burnaby.'"

"Good for her!" cried Will, waving his toasting
fork. Rosamund shifted herself to drop a swift
kiss of appreciation on her father's head and
then returned to her station.

"' Lewis and I are in Cannes,'" read on Mrs.
Burnaby. "' I have a French tutor for him. My
dear, the most marvellous man. Lewis just dotes
on him. The poor boy is still too delicate to go
to school. It's nothing that the doctors can lay
their hands on—just that he isn't robust like
other boys.'"

There was a faint retching noise from the
hearthrug, in which Will epitomised his feelings
as regards Master Lewis Vandermeyer.

"' I am taking Lewis to Switzerland for the
winter sports next week. M. Beaumont wants to
take a vacation then, and I was just wondering
whether you will let your two chicks come over
and join us as my guests. We are going to Reinigen. Now do please say yes.'"

"Mum!" Rosamund's eyes were like stars.
"Mummy, how simply glorious!"

"Winter sports!" Will gazed at a rapidly
blackening slice with unseeing eyes.

Mrs. Burnaby turned over another page.

"' This is very short notice but I'm afraid that's just my way of doing things. I never seem to be able to make up my mind till the last minute. I just won't take a refusal. I took such a fancy to those two sweet kids it would be a real pleasure to have them come. I've even wired to Reinigen to book their rooms. Grand Hotel, Reinigen, is the address. Lewis and I will be ready and waiting to welcome them. My kindest regards to that wonderful man your husband and we'll be hoping to see Rosamund and Will by January 1st. Ever your sincere friend, Mabel Vandermeyer.' "

"Well, well, well!" Mr. Burnaby laid down his cup and looked at his wife.

"Mummy, you couldn't refuse, could you?" pleaded Rosamund. "Oh, if only you knew how I've always longed to go to Switzerland!"

"Seems too good to be true," said Will. "Jolly nice of her."

"Do you think we can accept?" Mrs. Burnaby turned to her husband, who was watching the two eager faces on the hearthrug.

"I think so," he said slowly. "I am sure the invitation is very kindly meant. Mrs. Vandermeyer may feel indebted to me for winning that case over her English property, and wants to show her gratitude, but I think the fact that she wants young company for Lewis is the chief reason for the invitation."

"I wonder how much the journey will cost?" asked Mrs. Burnaby. "Can we manage that, David?"

"Good lord, I'd forgotten about that part," groaned Will."

"Don't worry." Mr. Burnaby smiled. "But I'm afraid there's no question of luxury travel, children. I can't run to sleepers. It'll be second class and sitting up all night."

"I don't care!" cried Rosamund. "Everything will be such fun. Oh, it's the most exciting thing that's ever happened to us! I suppose we shall have to be awfully nice to that little beast Loo-is. We can't let him be host and then tell him what we think of him, can we? Do you remember how he sat here and glowered at us and said he hated England?"

"No rose without a thorn," chanted Will. "Loo-is will be the fly in the ointment, the blot on the landscape, the spanner in the works, the . . . What on earth does it matter? He can't spoil the snow and the ski-ing and the skating, Gosh, isn't it terrific?"

"Clothes!" Rosamund turned tragic eyes to her mother and the two gazed at each other, mentally sizing up the possibilities of her meagre wardrobe.

"Never mind. We'll manage, Mum," she added swiftly, at sight of the furrow on Mrs. Burnaby's forehead. "As Will says, nothing, neither clothes nor Loo-is nor anything else can spoil the snow and the fun of it all. I shan't sleep a wink to-night!"

"Won't you crow over the Matthews girls at the party?" said Will wickedly.

"I wouldn't be so unchristian," Rosamund

retorted, her eyes dancing. "Will, do you realise we've only got four and a half days to wait! What a glorious American hustle it's going to be."

Rosamund snatched up the astonished Mrs. Fez-Fusby and cradled her in her arms.

"Darling Buzz, have you been listening?" she crooned. "Poor Buzz! You've never known what it was like to be skimming over the snow as though you had wings, with the sun shining above you and the mountains all round you. Nor have I, Fuzz-Buzz, not yet. But I'm going and I shall be doing it all! I'm the luckiest girl in the world and I want to go and shout it all up and down the streets."

"You'd soon be popped in the looney-bin at that rate, and then you wouldn't go to Switzerland at all," remarked the ever-practical Will. "Dad, is it on, quite definitely and irrevocably on?"

"Yes, Will."

Will heaved one vast sigh of content. Words failed him. "Come on, Rose," he remarked. "You ought to be fal-lalling for the Matthews. Bags I first bath."

*Master William Burnaby to Master Paul Stokes,
19 Briar Street, Cheltenham*

5 Beck Street,
Hampstead, N.W.3 *Jan. 27th*

DEAR PAUL,

I'm awfully sorry but I shan't be able to go

with you to Olympia next week. It was jolly nice
of your mother to ask me and I hope she won't
think it rude, but Rose and I are off to Switzerland. We're going to stay with some American
people at a place called Reinigen. I've looked it
out in Dad's old Baedeker. It sounds a marvellous
spot with cracking great mountains all round.
Do you think you'll be using your boots and
skates these hols? If not, I'd be jolly grateful to
borrow them. Peter Dunn has been frightfully
decent and lent me his ski-kit. I shall feel an
awful ass togged up in them. I expect I'll be
spending most of my time flat on my back.
What-ho for the wide open spaces!

I've just had my passport photo taken. It's
rather fetching. I look like Jack Ketch without
the black mask.

Well, all the best for the New Year, and tell
Mrs. Stokes I feel awfully bad about next
Thursday.

Yours ever,
WILL.

Miss Rosamund Burnaby to Miss Anne White,
The Close, Beddlington, Dorset

5 Beck Street,
Hampstead, N.W.3 Jan. 28th

DEAREST ANNE,

You'll never believe it! We're off to Switzerland
in three days' time! Do you remember the
American woman with the boy Lewis who came

to tea last summer while you were staying here? Well, it's her. I mean it's Mrs. Vandermeyer who has asked us out there. The letter came on Boxing Day and we're off on the 31st! You can't imagine the scramble we're having. Daddy has been a lamb about seeing to the tickets and money and things, but oh my dear, the clothes! Will was frightfully lucky. One boy has lent him a complete ski outfit and someone else is lending him skating boots and believe it or not, he's grown so much that he can get into Daddy's dinner jacket! But ME. I hadn't got a thing. But the age of miracles hasn't stopped, I can assure you. Dear old Miss Thacker from next door popped in and heard all about our going. She ran off straight away and fetched her own ski-suit. My dear, it was too embarrassing! The suit was a sort of knicker-bocker affair with puttees that you wound round your calves. It must have been made in the year one, but as luck would have it, the whole thing was simply tiny and I couldn't possibly have fitted into it. So we were able to thank her tremendously and pack it all up again, all but a lovely pair of boots and skates which fit me to a T. It was then that the miracles began to happen. She fumbled in her bag and murmured what a pleasure it had been to watch Will and me growing up and how nice it was to be seventeen and to have pretty clothes. Then the dear old thing insisted on writing me a cheque for fifty pounds then and there to spend on clothes for the trip! She did it so sweetly that it nearly made me cry when I was thanking her. We popped her into a taxi and insisted on her coming to choose the things with us, and I do really believe she enjoyed it almost as much as I did. So now you can picture me in a terrificly chic navy ski-suit, and oh, the evening dresses! Pink crêpe, with little pearls embroidered over the bodice, a heavenly yellow net, and a white lace. I feel quite light-headed. I suppose there is an earth still to tread on, but it's three days since my feet have touched it. Our address will be Grand Hotel, Reinigen. Do write to me if you can. My present address is Heaven House, Up-in-the-Clouds-lington, Nr. Bliss. What nonsense I'm writing! You mustn't mind. I've never been so excited in my life. En avant! Achtung! Swiss-wa'-hae!

Heaps of love,
ROSE.

CHAPTER TWO

FRESH FIELDS

THE remainder of the week sped past on wings. To Rosamund it was all part of the bliss of anticipation. Will was found to have packed several thrillers and his morse tapper but no pyjamas whatsoever. Rosamund was in a state of ecstasy that allowed for no coherent thought at all, and all Mrs. Burnaby's exhortations as to care of money and tickets and advice on procedure in a big hotel on her own floated in at one ear and out at the other.

Now the thirty-first had come. Mr. Burnaby was at the door with the car, and the great moment had arrived. Rosamund stood in the doorway, loth to start till she had savoured the moment to the full.

"Good-bye, darlings!" cried Mrs. Burnaby. "I wish I could come to the station too, but I must go and see Granny. Promise to write the moment you get there. Rosie darling, you will remember everything I've said? And promise not to sit about in the hotel in your thick clothes. The rooms are always so hot and you'll catch cold when you go out again."

"And change your socks if they're wet and brush your teeth twice a day and mind your table manners!" mocked Will. "Good-bye, Mum.

We'll look after ourselves. Don't you fret. All right, Dad. Just coming. Good-bye, Mrs. Elkin! Good-bye, everybody!"

Mrs. Elkin, wheezing somewhat after her climb up the area steps, thrust a paper parcel into Will's hand. "Now don't you go havin' anything to do with that there snow," she remarked. "Bye-bye, lovey."

Mrs. Elkin adored Will in spite of the hours she spent tidying up after him. Will's presence in any room resembled the passing of a young cyclone.

Even Mrs. Fez-Fusby had caught the excitement of the moment, which she expressed by a totally unprovoked attack on Major Mactavish's Scottie from No. 2.

It was a great send-off. All the neighbours had heard of the children's departure. Old Mr. Farman had put off his nap to wave from the windows of No. 3, Miss Matthews was leaning over her window-box, and Major Mactavish, having rescued his unfortunate hound from Mrs. Fez-Fusby's clutches, remained by the car to be in at the death, as he expressed it. Perhaps the happiness of the children's faces was sufficient to leave a reflected glow even on that dreary December morning.

It was only when the two were in the train, and Mr. Burnaby had hurried off to his office, that Rosamund felt a little thrill almost of fear.

"Will, you've got the tickets, haven't you?"

"'Course I have. Inside coat pocket. Safe as houses," said Will.

The train changed note to a dull roar as it made its way over the Thames. Soon the factories were replaced by row upon row of small houses and back gardens, only in their turn to be left behind for the green fields and orchards of Kent.

"Will, what do you feel like?" asked Rosamund earnestly.

Will looked at his sister with tolerant amusement. He never shared her passion for analysing all her feelings.

"Jolly hungry," he said. "I wish I'd eaten more breakfast."

"There's a restaurant car," suggested Rosamund doubtfully.

Will allowed the suggestion to drop. Neither admitted it, but they were both feeling slightly lost and shy. This was the first time they had ever travelled on their own except for the regular short trips to and from school. The situation resolved itself by Will's coming upon Mrs. Elkin's parcel in his haversack. Joy of joys, it contained jam puffs made by Mrs. Elkin's own hands, which had a magic touch upon the pastry board.

They munched gratefully as the cold grey landscape passed by.

Rosamund looked with some disappointment at their fellow-passengers. They consisted of two French girls, rather dowdily dressed, a middle-aged and most obvious Englishwoman with a pile of newspapers which she was reading as conscientiously as though her future depended on their perusal, and a fat little man who might be

a Russian prince in disguise or just as likely a
commercial traveller from Tooting.

However, her imagination, as usual, came to
her rescue, and before they had thundered through
Ashford Junction she had made up the life story
of the middle-aged Englishwoman who, on being
disappointed in love, was forced to fill her mind
all day long, year in, year out, with newspapers,
to prevent her heart from breaking. She had just
begun on the little fat man, who must be quite
definitely in the Secret Service, when Will's voice
roused her.

"I think we're coming into Dover."

The train slowed to a standstill and poured its
passengers on to the bleak platform.

The formalities were easier to manage than
they had feared, and before long the two found
themselves climbing the gangway of the stout
channel vessel.

"I—say, after this—we—shall have—to talk
French," panted Will, struggling to take off his
cap in apology to an elderly lady without dropping his suitcases. "You can do the parlez-
vousing, my girl. Gosh, this is a trim little craft!
D'you think we shall be sea-sick? Suppose we
ought to have kept those jam-puffs till afterwards. Looks pretty choppy to me."

Most of the passengers had hurried down below,
but the two elected to stay on deck. Neither of
them had ever left England before, and every hoot
of the siren, every fresh move on the sailors' part,
was of deep interest. They watched the boat-train
arriving, and with it the first-class passengers.

Groups of young people, laughing and talking and obviously very much at home, poured up the gangway. Drifts of conversation wafted by concerning what old Henry did on the Bergheim run last year and the marvels of the snow at Pontresina. "My dear, it's too divine. You simply must go." A fair girl brushed past with two attendant swains.

Rosamund glanced at Will to see whether he was feeling quite as young and out of his element as she felt at sight of these young lordlings in their leather jackets and casual scarves. Would she ever be able to talk lightly of the respective merits of the great hotels and the relative excellence of the ski runs? No, Will was quite indifferent to it all. But men were like that. They cared about things so much more than people. There was Will, absorbed in watching the men loosening the mooring ropes, while she was envying the fair girl's fur coat. How horrid of her! She moved over to Will and watched the quay drifting slowly away from them.

Once out at sea, the cold drove even Rosamund and Will into the crowded saloon. Quite half the passengers on the boat seemed to be going winter-sporting. There was an anxious young man with a red nose, rounding up a large and elusive party from Fenn's tourist agency. There was a great deal of laughter and swopping of reminiscences. By half-way over, however, the saloon had emptied considerably. Rosamund felt a most unchristian gleam of satisfaction as, passing through the ladies' cabins, she saw the fair owner of the fur coat groaning on a bunk. She and Will congratulated each other on being excellent sailors and toasted themselves in ginger beer, fortified by ham sandwiches.

As they neared the French coast, the sea became rougher. One or two more till then merry-makers hastily left the saloon. A ham sandwich slithered from Rosamund's plate and lodged itself on the corduroy calf that belonged to the man seated immediately on her left. His back was towards her and as yet he was quite unaware of the accident.

Rosamund looked cautiously round. Will, her usual ally, had unfortunately just gone on deck to watch for the French coast. However, no one was looking. She was still extremely hungry and the sandwich would be none the worse for its sojourn on that new and smart-looking corduroy. She drummed a nonchalant little ditty on the table with one hand, while her other hand slid under the table. Feverishly she sought for the softness of the velvet. Her bearings must be wrong. She decided to risk a quick glance.

She turned, only to find herself looking into the face of the owner of the corduroys. He was quite a young man, with a mass of thick fair hair and blue eyes that were gazing steadily at her. He looked quite grave, yet there was an unmistakable twitch about his mouth and a definite twinkle in his eyes.

Rosamund felt herself go scarlet. Had he seen her hand? Where was the luckless ham sandwich? Perhaps he merely wished to scrape acquaintance with her, in which case she would freeze him with a glance. However, she took the weaker line of defence and turned her head stonily towards the stout French lady on her other side.

"Excuse me."

Rosamund turned to find the blue eyes still twinkling at her.

"If you wish to pick my pockets, I keep them here." He patted the enormous pockets of his overcoat.

"I—it—I mean—I had lost something."

The young man clicked his tongue solicitously. "You must allow me to help you. Is it Mademoiselle's handbag or her gloves?"

"It really doesn't matter. They were only an old pair." The lie left her lips almost before Rosamund knew it. It was too late to retract now. She cast an anguished glance down the saloon to see if Will had reappeared.

The young man was still all concern. Rosamund, in spite of her distress, found herself wondering what nationality he was. He spoke perfect English, yet with a faint lilt in the slow, pleasant voice.

"If you push back your chair, I will make an expedition under the table," he offered.

"No!" It was almost a wail. If he were to kneel there, he would assuredly kneel on the sandwich. "I'm—I'm quite glad to lose them. I—I—hated them."

The young man had risen as he spoke and pulled his own chair forward. His eyes for a moment were riveted on some object at his feet.

"If they really are of no consequence, I will search no further," he said quietly. With a little bow he picked up his despatch-case and walked towards the door.

At last Rosamund could look under the table. Yes, there lay the sandwich, indubitably he had seen it. Why had she told all those ridiculous lies? What must he have thought of her? She imagined to herself how the girl in the fur coat would have dealt with the same situation. "Excuse me, but I've dropped a sandwich on your leg. Hold still a moment, will you?" Just as easy as that, it would have been. She wondered who he could be. He had looked at her so differently after he had seen through her silly pretence. She picked up her coat and determined to forget all about it. She made her way up on deck to join Will, who with a crowd of hardy enthusiasts were watching the grey harbour of Calais emerging from the mist like a wraith of its own self.

Even Will's calm slightly forsook him when faced with the shouts of the French porters and the general hurly-burly of arrival. But by following the queue, they at last found themselves free of the Customs and ejected on to the platform, there rather forlornly to search for their second-class carriage.

Their seats were found at last. Rosamund had tried out her French on several officials, but unfortunately her questions had provoked such a torrent of fatherly advice, that she was quite incapable of understanding. Will, in truly British style, flatly refused to speak French at all, but

by demanding their way in English, had succeeded where poor Rosamund had failed.

The carriage was comfortable enough, and
they found that by great good luck there were
to be only two other occupants, a very small
dark man buried in French newspapers, and, by
a coincidence, the same bald-headed fat man who
had been in their carriage on the way to Dover.
This coincidence broke the ice, and by the time
Calais had faded into the dusk, the three had
become excellent friends. Alas for Rosamund's
theories! The fat man proved to be no Secret
Service agent, but a Mr. Smith who travelled all
over Europe for an engineering firm, with a wife
and four children in Birmingham. He insisted
on their having dinner with him, and won their
admiration by ordering the food in the most
perfect French.

Once more Rosamund's heart sang with adventures to come, as she sipped the red wine that
Mr. Smith pressed upon them and her fork made
voyages of exploration into her pile of hors
d'œuvre. She looked blissfully up and down the
tables of the restaurant car. Will was engrossed
in a technical question with Mr. Smith on the
building of cranes, so she was at her own disposal.
She glanced over Will's curly mop, past Mr.
Smith's aimiable head, to all the other heads
bent earnestly over their food. Here and there a
white napkin was tucked into a shirt-front, here
and there a waiter was obsequiously pointing out
the choice wines on the list.

"This is me, Rosamund Burnaby," said Rosamund to herself. "I'm dining on a French train with someone we'd never met till a few hours ago, with three brand-new evening dresses in my suitcase and a whole fortnight's holiday to come. There'll never be a moment like this again."

Only one slight cloud hung on the horizon, a cloud that she tried to banish angrily from her mind. It was occasioned by the vision of a pair of very blue eyes that had lost all interest in her.

It was ten o'clock, and Mr. Smith had escorted them back to their carriage.

"How does one get comfortable for the night?" asked Rosamund rather faintly.

Mr. Smith smiled cheerfully. "One doesn't," he said. "The aim is to be no more uncomfortable than need be. We're lucky to be only four in the carriage. Two last-minute cancellations, I suppose. Now, let's put all the suitcases in a row down the middle of the carriage. The great thing is to make them up to the level of the seats."

Under this experienced guidance, a sort of vast Bed of Ware was created, the suitcases being softened by any available coats not already destined for pillows. The little foreigner in the far corner made no offer to assist. He seemed to take no interest in the proceedings, but sat quietly watching the passers-by in the corridor. Rosamund's eyes fell on his hands. They were the only remarkable feature about him, as small as a woman's and curiously white. They were so surprising on that small sallow man, that Rosamund found herself constantly glancing at them, almost as though they were a separate entity in the carriage.

When the arrangements were completed, Mr. Smith proceeded to loosen his collar, remove his gold-rimmed glasses, fold his coat under his head, and prepare himself for sleep. Rosamund, being small, found no great difficulty in fitting herself in. Her last memory was the sight of Will in comical dismay, trying to telescope his length into an impossible series of curves and angles. The light from the corridor shone on the dark man's hands, as he sat quietly and expressionless in his corner. There was something a little sinister in the quietness of that man. Rosamund smiled sleepily to herself. She could almost hear Will saying, "Don't be an ass, Rose. You're always imagining things." Silly of her to think of a word like sinister. Sinister meant something evil. What had that little man to do with evil? What was there about this whole trip but sun and snow and fun and excitement? She liked the dud-dud-dud-dud of the train. How it rocked. Dud-dud-dud-dud, dud-dud-dud-dud.

Rosamund awoke with a start. She had been dreaming that the fair young man was leaning over her with a ham sandwich on a string. She saw with relief that it was only Mr. Smith, leaning over her to pull up the blinds. He was already shaven and neat and smiling aimiably through his gold-rimmed glasses. Will was still asleep, looking rather like a problem out of a geometry book. The small dark man still sat upright in his corner.

"Seven o'clock of the morning and a happy New Year!" said Mr. Smith. "We get to Berne at eight, you know. We're well over the frontier."

Rosamund jumped to her feet.

"Happy New Year!" she cried. "Oh dear, I wish I'd woken earlier."

"You wouldn't have seen much if you had," said Mr. Smith. "It's only just getting light."

Rosamund looked round her. The train had sprung into life again. People were hurrying up and down the corridor or waiting in a resigned queue their turn to wash or shave. In the faint daylight she could see the snowy slopes on either side of the railway. She looked in vain for the sharp mountain peaks that she had pictured, but Mr. Smith explained that she must be patient as they were still only in the lowlands.

She roused Will unmercifully to look at the scenery. Poor Will had suffered for his five-foot ten inches, and he woke protesting that he had never so much as closed an eye all night. However, his aches and pains were soon forgotten in the excitement of their arrival in Berne, where they were to change for Reinigen. Here they were more than ever glad of Mr. Smith's company, for the kind little man refused to go to his hotel until he had given Rosamund and Will their first taste of the glories of a Swiss breakfast. He might have baked the delicious white rolls himself and been the owner of every jam factory in Switzerland to judge by his pleasure over the children's raptures. Everything delighted them. The cleanness of the station, with its network of electric wires overhead that did away with the steam and dirt of an English station, the porters in their neat blue uniforms with their luggage trolleys like miniature trains. They watched with amusement the same party from Fenn's Tours being rounded up by the same young man with the red nose, who looked more like a distracted hen than ever.

It was with real sorrow that the two parted from Mr. Smith, when he had put them into the train for Interbrunnen, their next change, and assured himself that their tickets were all in order.

"I never knew guardian angels wore spectacles and had bald heads," said Rosamund as she leaned out of the window to say good-bye. "Whatever should we have done without him? Every one seems to talk German. This is where you take over, Willie, my boy. You learn it at school."

"We'll get around with English, don't you fret," said Will, who, unlike Rosamund, never met troubles half-way. "We've got a couple of hours of this and then for the funicular. That'll be no end interesting. I want to see how they work the cables."

The train wound on, making a slow ascent through the winding valleys. Here and there a small village peeped out from under its blanket of snow. Rosamund darted from side to side of the carriage, keeping up a running commentary on the scenery, and constantly endangering the market baskets belonging to the two elderly Swiss women who occupied the other corner seats.

After a few gleams, the sun had retired firmly behind a bank of clouds, and before long a few snowflakes began to fall. Faster they fell and faster, till the whole landscape had narrowed to the swirling white flakes outside the window.

There were several halts where unfamiliar names loomed suddenly forth on their placards. At length the train drew up at what appeared a slightly larger station.

"I can't see the name anywhere!" cried Rosamund hecticly. "Will, we simply must ask someone! Go on, ask those two women in German if this is Interbrunnen."

"Certainly," said Will, rather surprisingly. He lifted his cap and smiled charmingly at the two stolid figures.

"Interbrunnen?" he asked.

"Ja, ja!" they nodded.

Will looked triumphantly at Rosamund. "Wonderful help to know a language, isn't it?" he remarked.

They descended into the narrow world of snow and looked up and down the platform. A number of other people had clambered out and were hurrying towards an exit. A porter was handling a load of skis. There was much laughter among a group of English in ski-ing kit.

The exit led to the funicular, a three-compartmented contraption like a train in a nightmare, as Rosamund described it, set at a terrifying angle against the hillside. They sat down on the wooden seat of the third compartment, which rapidly filled with the ski-ers they had seen on the plat-form. Their conversation was Greek to Rosa-mund and Will, all about the technicalities of a ski race that was to be run the next day and the relative chances of who would win.

"You ought to have a jolly good chance, Donald," called out a pretty girl from the corner. "You beat Pat's record, didn't you?"

Donald was a tall youth with an impossible scarf and a very off-hand manner.

"Might. You never know," he drawled. "All depends if Otto von Vierling turns up. His name's down for it. Rumour has it he's arriving to-day. Haven't an earthly in that case. He won the championship last year. International class, you know."

"Darn fine athlete," muttered another young man. "If this snow clears by to-morrow, con-ditions will be perfect. I'm going in for the slalom, by the way. Not a chance in a million of winning, but good fun, what?"

"I say, you're keeping the waltzes for me to-night, aren't you, Prue?" called out a leather jerkin, topped by a rather pimply young man with an enormous moustache.

"Good lord, you're the third person I've promised them to!" called back the pretty girl. "My memory just simply doesn't exist. I can't even remember who the other chaps are."

"Affected ass," muttered Will of the pretty girl. Rosamund smiled, but again a faint wave of depression passed over her. It was rather like being a small girl on her first day at school.

She looked over the head of the leather jerkin into the carriage in front. She noticed for the first time that the small dark man whom they had lost sight of at Berne was sitting facing her. She could only see his head and shoulders. He was muffled in an overcoat with a large fur collar. A curious little tingle that was neither cold nor excitement, but more of a vague fear, passed through her. Perhaps those white hands of his had reminded her of something that she had once read and forgotten, something unpleasant.

Just then a bell rang, there was a sudden jerk, and they were off.

The snow was too thick to see to any distance. They could only look down at the track beside them that seemed all but perpendicular. Before long, the rail branched and the little downward car passed by. Up and up into the silent world of snow they were borne. Rosamund's imagination had already carried her almost to the top of the Jungfrau, when there was another jolt and the upper platform was reached.

Out tumbled the ski-ers. There were more shouts and chaffing and in twos and threes they disappeared into the white world beyond.

"Do you think any one will have come to meet us?" asked Rosamund anxiously. "I think I'd be glad even to see Loo-is just now."

Will reluctantly dragged himself away from the machinery and joined her in the little waiting-room.

"What a fusser you are!" he remarked calmly. "Look!"

There, outside in the snow, stood a porter bearing the title Grand Hotel on his peaked cap. Rosamund gave a little cry of thankfulness and delight, for behind him stood a sleigh, drawn by a sleek brown pony.

"Mees Bairnaby? Meester Bairnaby? Will you come, plees?" The porter consulted a card and smiled at the two.

A moment later, with bells jangling gaily, they were driving through the scurrying snow.

Reinigen as a village was disappointing, as it had grown up only round the sports centre. The main street was lined with shops showing gay Swiss scarves and wood-carvings to catch the tourist's eye, or sports goods. There were one or two cafés and pensions, and standing on the hill above the village was the Grand Hotel, an immense building of grey stone.

A few moments later, they had left the outside world, the hotel doors had swung to behind them, and they stood in the entrance hall, an immense room decorated with chamois heads, a red Turkey carpet under their feet.

Rosamund pinched Will's arm to reassure herself.

"Will, do you realise where we are?" she whispered. "We're in Switzerland, Willie! We're actually definitely and unmistakably here."

CHAPTER THREE

INITIATION

"Now, chicks, isn't this just lovely? Isn't it wonderful?"

It was lunch-time the following day. Mrs. Vandermeyer sat between Rosamund and Will, her small fat fingers crumbling her roll while she smiled happily at her guests. Mrs. Vandermeyer was a dear, both had already decided that. She might be rather tiresome, she might be a little too brightly dressed and far, far too rich, but it would be impossible to be really angry with her. She breathed good nature from the top of her too-brilliant hair to the soles of her too-tight French shoes. Mrs. Vandermeyer enjoyed life and was so childishly pleased with her own wealth, that somehow the world smiled with her rather than at her. And for Mrs. Vandermeyer to enjoy life, it was necessary that her friends should enjoy it too, and her generosity knew no bounds.

"My, my, this is great!" she went on. "What a shame poor Lewis is in bed with a cold. He's been living for your arrival, just living for it. My, Will, what a great big boy you are! Rosamund, I can see you're going to be the belle of the ball to-night. They'll all be crazy about you. Garçong, a little more chicken!"

Mrs. Vandermeyer's eyes roved round the tables. She waved her fat little be-ringed hand once or twice and smiled.

"I must have you meet some of the folks," she said. "Now, tell me, what did you do with yourselves this morning?"

"We skated," said Rosamund. "It was awful fun. I've done a bit at home, but never on a gorgeous rink like this."

"I spent the morning trying to go backwards," said Will. "Can't imagine why anybody wants to really, but I suppose there's a sort of gloomy satisfaction about it. I shall strap a cushion on to-morrow," he added.

Rosamund ate her chicken in happy silence, while Mrs. Vandermeyer prattled on about the hotel and her own health and M. Beaumont and the wonderful French that Lewis now talked, and the hundred and one small matters that occupied her comfortable small mind.

It had been a wonderful morning. They had awoken to brilliant sunshine and a world so carpeted in dazzling white that the pine-trees were dropping under their burden of snow. The only sounds were the sh-sh of the men's shovels clearing the skating rink or the occasional chatter of some early riser, determined to make the most of the day.

Will and Rosamund had breakfasted alone, as Mrs. Vandermeyer never rose till lunch-time and Lewis was still in bed with a cold and had shown no desire for visitors. After this they had made their way to the skating rink, where several early birds had already congregated. Rosamund blessed her stars that she could skate passably well. Will was quite impervious to his shortcomings and cheerfully fell about, thereby making friends with most of their fellow-skaters. It had been delightful, and every one had been most kind and friendly. By dint of help from either side, Will had been towed like the *Queen Mary* with two attendant tugs round the rink, till by the end of the morning he had made quite creditable progress.

Mrs. Vandermeyer broke off the recital of the probable cause of her last fit of palpitations, to wave to a middle-aged couple who had just come in.

"There go Colonel and Mrs. Parker," she announced. "He runs the sports here and all the entertainments. Such a nice man, vurry distinguished. Ah, there's Miss Drover! She writes books. A vurry clever woman, I'm told. That's Mr. Palmer. He's the padre here. Such a charming man. I met him last year. And, my dears, his sermons, his sermons! It just brings tears to your eyes to hear such beautiful thoughts."

Mrs. Vandermeyer gazed at her second helping of chicken as though the beautiful thought had materialised on the plate before her.

"We've hired skis and we're going to have a shot at the nursery slopes this afternoon," volunteered Will.

"My dears, the energy of you! I wish Lewis were half as energetic, I do indeed. Well, honeys, we'll meet for dinner, eh? I'm going to have a

little game of Bridge. Gorgeous day, what a
gorgeous day! I simply adore the snow. Have a
good time, chicks."

With which Mrs. Vandermeyer cheerfully
turned her back on the snow and was soon
closeted in the Bridge room, there to lose heavily
with the greatest good humour.

Feeling slightly self-conscious in their ski-suits,
Rosamund and Will shouldered their skis and
made their way along the track to the nursery
slopes at the back of the hotel.

On their way their attention was drawn to
what looked like a pair of disembodied skis
waving wildly in the air. Will stopped to investigate this phenomenon, and came upon an elderly
man who had fallen into a snowdrift. He seemed
quite undismayed, and, catching hold of Will's
proffered ski-stick, pulled himself up, shook
himself like a dog, and, thanking Will for
his assistance, plodded up the slope again.

Rosamund and Will followed up the path, their
eyes turned wistfully on a few of the practised
who were perfecting turns with great ease and
nonchalance. Arrived at the top of the slope,
Will helped Rosamund to fasten her skis, while
the elderly man gave words of advice.

"Not so difficult as you might think," he said.
"Confidentially speaking, I'd never tried it myself
till a few days ago. Always wanted to ski ever
since I was a boy. I keep a little café on the Great
North Road—wonderful spot for business. I've
been saving up for this little jaunt. It's what I've

always wanted and here I am. It's not so hard. Weight forward—watch me. Here we go."

Rosamund and Will watched. Gradually, as the unfortunate man gathered speed, his weight receded farther and farther backwards.

"He's nearly over!" cried Rosamund.

"Good lord, he's gone into the same snow-drift!" said Will.

"Come on, Rose. Let's get cracking."

The next hour was hard labour, but by the end of it, both Rosamund and Will could progress down the hill without falling over. At intervals they went to the rescue of the elderly gentleman, who invariably ended his descent either in his favourite snowdrift or twisted into such contortions that he was incapable of unwinding himself. Always he picked himself up undaunted and smiling.

"Always wanted to do this," he would murmur as he started toiling again up the slope.

At last Rosamund felt that she could do no more. Flushed, exhausted and triumphant, she sat down on a bench above the slopes. The sun was growing low over the great white bulk of mountain that lay beyond the valley. A faint tinge that was to grow to a sunset glow had lighted up the jagged range beyond. She drew in great breaths of the tingling air.

"Heaven!" she murmured aloud. "Sheer heaven."

All at once she wondered whether the clear light had conjured up a mirage. For coming slowly up the path, a pair of skis on his shoulder,

was the tall figure of the young man on the boat.
Rosamund's heart missed a beat. There was no
doubt about it. Flight was impossible, so she
must brazen this out. He might not even remember her. She watched him slowly mounting the
path till he was almost level with her. He paused
and smiled. It was without doubt a smile of
recognition.

"May I join you?" he asked. "It's a superb
view from here, isn't it?"

"Wonderful. Haven't we met before? Ah yes,
surely it was on the boat." Rosamund's voice
was a study in casualness. "Are you staying at
the Grand?"

"I have just arrived. I stayed the night with
friends in Berne."

There was a pause.

"Are you fond of ski-ing?" he asked.

"I only started this afternoon," said Rosamund.
"I think it's tremendous fun. Have you come
up here to try? I know how to fit the skis on if
I can help you."

"That's very kind of you," he murmured. "I
couldn't think of troubling you."

"I really don't mind." Rosamund was slightly
inflated with her afternoon's success, and truth
to tell, was longing to show off her prowess to
another beginner.

"If I were you, I should stick to that side of
the slope," she advised. "There are some awful
bumps over there. I still can't get over them
without falling down. Keep your weight well
forward. It's quite easy, honestly."

The fair young man bent down over his skis. His voice sounded slightly muffled.

"In case I never return from this wild venture, may I first know your name?" he asked.

"Rosamund Burnaby."

"Rosamund Burnaby." He looked up swiftly to survey her. "It suits you." His skis were in place, yet he lingered.

"It's quite all right, really!" encouraged Rosamund.

He opened his mouth as though to speak, then changed his mind. He drew a small pattern with his ski-stick on the snow.

"In case I've . . ."

There was the sound of voices on the path below. Two ski-ers climbed rapidly towards them.

"Otto!" yelled one. "They're all waiting for you!"

"Good lord, I'd forgotten!" murmured the fair young man.

"They're polishing off the heats this afternoon!" called up the other.

With an exclamation of annoyance, the young man pulled on his ski cap and fastened it under his chin.

"Right. I'll be with you," he called. "If you will excuse me, Mademoiselle . . ."

There was a crunch of ice as his sticks bit into the pathway. He shot forward on to the slope, not on to the course prescribed by Rosamund, but the steepest and most direct way to the road below. A perfect turn here, a whirr of snow, and he had passed out of sight, skimming the ground like a darting bird.

Rosamund gave a little strangled gasp.

The elderly man had seated himself on the bench beside her.

"Beautiful sight!" he murmured. "What a ski-er!"

"Who—who is he?" stammered Rosamund.

"Don't you know?" said the elderly man. "That's Otto von Vierling. He's an international ski-er. Well, well, one more try before tea. Here we go."

Rosamund watched him descend slowly and resignedly till he collapsed into his usual snow-drift. Her mind was seething with fury against the fair young man. That he should have deliberately misled her, that he should have allowed her to make a fool of herself again! She blushed hotly to think of the advice she had given him. However, on second thoughts, Rosamund was just enough to admit that he hadn't deliberately misled her. It had all been the fault of her wretched imagination. Just because he had arrived at the nursery slopes, she had straight-way pictured herself teaching him to ski. It was horrible. She could never face him again. He would always be laughing at her.

All her triumph gone, she followed Will back to the hotel for tea, listening with only half an ear to his explanations about stem-turns and his plans for new achievements the next day. Even the chocolate éclairs did not quite blot out the chagrin of her stupid mistake. Otto von Vierling.

Was he German? Swiss? What could he be? She noticed that the little dark man from the train was sitting at the table opposite to them. He had been joined now by another man, a swarthy long-nosed man, who jerked himself about as he talked, in strange contrast to the stillness of the other. So that was why the little dark man had come to the Grand Hotel, to meet this friend. She wondered why they had chosen this particular hotel. No two men ever looked less like ardent winter-sporters.

Suddenly she drew back against the curtains, praying that she was shielded from the door. For standing in the doorway, chatting with a group of young men, stood Otto von Vierling.

Rosamund could never tell what made her glance at that precise moment at the small dark man and his friend. To her surprise, the small man was leaning forward, for the first time with an expression of interest in his face. His white hands were clasped tightly together, a newspaper crushed between them. She followed his eyes. They were fixed intently on Otto von Vierling.

"You see, you must learn to stem or you can never regulate your speed," expounded Will, who with his usual thoroughness could now neither think nor talk of anything but ski-ing. "It's only a case of control. I say, you're not listening!"

Rosamund turned to him with a slight start.

"Yes, I am, honestly," she said swiftly. Bother her imagination. What a pity that she couldn't control that by stemming, she thought ruefully.

Why had that word sinister run through her brain again at sight of those clasped white hands? Why had she wanted to leap up and warn Otto that he was being watched? What could be more natural than the little man's interest in an international ski-er? Why did those white hands haunt her so?

She was roused from her thoughts by a new entry into the lounge. It was a boy of about Will's age, with a pasty face and a discontented twist to his mouth.

Rosamund nudged Will.

"Loo-is, by Jingo!" murmured Will. "From beasties and from all things that go bump in the night, Good Lord deliver us! Well, we should be in good old Hampstead but for Loo-is, so come on and let's do our stuff."

Rosamund accordingly touched the boy on the arm as he passed their table. A quick look almost of annoyance flashed over him.

"Oh, you're Rosamund and Will, aren't you?" he remarked. "Ma said you were coming. Guess I'd better have tea with you."

This was hardly the speech expected from one who had been "living" for their arrival. However, the boy looked so sick of himself and of the world in general, that Rosamund instantly resolved that he must become their mission for the next fortnight. Gaily she talked of their journey and the hotel and the snow. But no answering spark could be roused in Lewis's face, no promise could be extracted from him that he would come ski-ing with them the next morning. He resisted all attempts to be drawn on any subject with a sullenness that dried up even Rosamund's ready tongue.

At last she and Will escaped on the pretext of having to write letters home, leaving Master Lewis and his ill-manners to their own devices.

It soon became evident that Lewis's sulks were permanent. At dinner it became positively painful. It was a dance night, and every one had dressed accordingly.

Mrs. Vandermeyer had appeared in a creation of flaming scarlet that was startling to say the least of it.

"Ma, whatever made you put on that thing? It's fierce," remarked her loving son as they sat down to the meal.

Mrs. Vandermeyer's fat face quivered with disappointment.

"Don't you like it, honey?" she said. "It came from Estelle's in Cannes. They said it was as chic as chic."

"What beautiful material!" put in Rosamund quickly, whereupon Mrs. Vandermeyer brightened immediately.

"Now, what are we going to eat? Lewis, you order. I'd like Rosamund and Will to hear how your French has come on. M. Beaumont is a wonderful teacher and Lewis has such an ear for languages."

Lewis glowered.

"American is good enough for me," he growled. "I told you the waiter speaks English, Ma."

"I know, honey," soothed Mrs. Vandermeyer. "But I just adore to hear you talk French."

"Aw, can't you leave me alone, Ma?" said Lewis fiercely. "I hate rotten old French anyway."

It was a difficult meal. Rosamund and Will made conversation valiantly, but Mrs. Vandermeyer's pathetic pride in Lewis made her turn constantly to him for him to air his knowledge or give an opinion, always with the same result. Lewis either glowered in silence or flatly contradicted her. The others were thankful when they were able to adjourn to the ballroom.

Lewis, after one look at the crowd, muttered something about a detective book and fled. Mrs. Vandermeyer gallantly elected to stay to " start you off, honeys," as she expressed it, but the sight of her longing glances towards the Bridge room soon made Rosamund assure her that they would be quite happy on their own. The question was settled by kindly Colonel Parker, who had caught sight of Rosamund's wistful face, and promptly bore her off to introduce her to partners. Will, relieved of his duties, made his escape to talk ski-ing with another non-dancer whom he had spotted supporting the wall opposite.

Only once did she see Otto von Vierling. He was standing in the doorway talking to the proprietor. She was whirled down the room by her partner, and when she looked again, the doorway was empty.

She crept up to bed in the small hours of the morning and leaned her flushed face out of the window. It was moonlight, crystal-clear and sparkling, the blue shadows of the snow turning to purple under the trees. There was a faint waft of pine in the icy air. For once Rosamund's mind could conjure up no words. The beauty of the night could only be felt, never fitted into the empty shapes of words. She lay in bed watching the starry sky, a magic curtain stretched across her window. Why had Otto von Vierling not come to the dance? Was he bored with the people in the hotel? She tried to conjure up his face as she had often done with other faces. For an instant it rose quite clearly before her, then it was blotted out, blotted out by a pair of white hands, hands that held a crushed newspaper between them. The sudden vision was unpleasant. Resolutely she pushed it from her mind, youth and her weariness coming to her help. Soon all visions had faded into a dreamless sleep.

Miss Rosamund Burnaby to Mrs. Burnaby,
5 Beck Street, Hampstead, N.W.3

Grand Hotel,
Reinigen, *Jan.* 7*th*

DEAREST MUMMY AND DADDY,

Do you realise we've been here a week to-day? I've been a pig not to have written you longer letters, but though it sounds silly, I never seem to get a moment. Never mind, this shall be a nice fat one.

Well, everything is just what I'd expected only about fifty times nicer. There are nearly two hundred people in the hotel and I think we know most of them already. Winter-sporting is such a lovely friendly thing. When you've picked some-body's ski out of their right ear, or they've sat down on you on the skating rink, you can't help feeling that you've been friends for life. Will is quite crazy about ski-ing and getting awfully good. Most of the men take it terribly seriously and they're always having competitions and things. But the men are funniest about the curling. Have you ever watched any? It's like a sort of bowls on ice. You see nice fat old gentle-men tearing along in front of the stone thing they throw, brushing away at the ice for dear life with a little straw broom. Woe betide any one who laughs. It's a VERY SERIOUS GAME.

Some of the people here are so funny. There's a little man called Mr. Brett who runs a café on the Great North Road. He skis all day long and he never gets any better at all. He's so sweet about it. He and Will play backgammon together on dance nights. Colonel Parker is a great friend of mine. He runs the games and things here and pops about blowing whistles and giving orders just as though he were on the parade ground again. He pulls his moustaches and his eyes send out sparks (isn't that what a colonel's eyes always do in the best novels?) but he's simply sweet about seeing that nobody gets left out and every-body's enjoying themselves.

One of the nicest people is a Miss Drover. She's quite elderly but is so amusing to talk to. You see her and her friend, Miss Fox-Strangways, striding along for miles in their snow-boots. They go for what Miss Drover calls " a jolly trudge " every morning and every afternoon. I believe Miss Fox-Strangways writes poetry and Miss Drover writes books on travel. Then there's a terrible little man called Mr. Ivor, who sits in the lounge and tries to catch someone to tell all about his illnesses. He says he's had more diseases than any one of his acquaintance and is terribly proud of them! I had the life history of his liver before lunch. A jolly good trudge with Miss Drover is what he needs. Then there's a very nice professor from Berne called Dr. Schlacht, who talks the most priceless English. There are a certain number of French here and some Belgians, but there are far more British than anything else.

Mrs. Vandermeyer is being very sweet to us— when we see her! She raves all day about the beautiful mountain air, but so far I don't think she's even put her nose outside the front door. She plays Bridge all day long. Loo-is is even more of a menace than ever. Will and I have tried terribly hard to be friendly to him, but it's like trying to be friendly with a stone wall. He won't ski and he won't skate and he won't dance, and goes round looking as though he hated everybody, including himself! I'm sure he's a phs—psy—physo—no, that's wrong—psychologi- cal case, had his rattle taken away when he was a baby or something. I feel we shan't have earned our board if we can't de-Loo-is Loo-is! Any suggestions gratefully received.

Oh dear, I really must stop. I promised Will to go and watch the jumping championships this morning. We're taking picnic lunches as the jumping is right away up on the hill. There's going to be an ice carnival to-night. Darlings, I didn't know life *could* be such fun!

Heaps and heaps of love,

Rose.

PS.—I've got a thing like an enormous white bolster on my bed instead of an eiderdown. I thought one of the mountains had walked in at the window when I woke up the first morning.

PPS.—There's a marvellous ski-er here called Otto von Vierling. We met on the boat coming over. He looks rather nice.

Postcard from Mr. William Burnaby to Mrs. Elkin, 5 Beck Street, Hampstead, N.W.3.

Grand Hotel,
Reinigen, *Jan.* 7th

Thanks awfully for those jam puffs. This is a view of the Enghorn. It's a socking great brute. Has snow on it all the year round. Ski-ing's grand. Will you look in the back scullery cupboard? I put a couple of dead mice in there out of the attic trap for Fuzz-Buzz. They'll be getting a bit ripe. Rose sends her love.

Yours affectly.,

Will.

Mrs. Vandermeyer to Mrs. Burnaby, 5 *Beck Street,*
*Hampstead, N.W.*3

> Grand Hotel,
> Reinigen, *Jan.* 7*th*

MY DEAR MRS. BURNABY,

Just two words to tell you that Lewis and I are just crazy about your two. Rosamund is the sweetest thing I've ever seen and it won't be the fault of the young men here if she doesn't get her head turned! I'm sure Will and Lewis are going to be the best of friends. It's just what my Lewis needs. He's so reserved and shy. He should have a boy of his age to rag about with.

Will you please remember me to that lovely man, your husband, and believe me.

> Yours very sincerely,
> MABEL VANDERMEYER.

CHAPTER FOUR

A FAMILY HISTORY

FOLLOWING a long and straggling procession of spectators, Rosamund and Will climbed up the path behind the hotel to the site of the ski-jumps. The gentle fall of the nursery slopes lay to their right. To the left, the ground fell steeply away a thousand feet or more to the foot of the valley, where the little mountain train wound past with its load of human fodder for the funicular. There, a few hundred feet down the slope, a platform had been built. Above it, the steep slope had been beaten smooth, below it the ground sank away to the valley at a terrifying angle.

"You don't mean to say they jump off that platform!" gasped Rosamund.

"They do indeed," said Colonel Parker, who was standing near, a stop-watch in hand. "Wonderful nerve those fellows have. Style counts too as well as distance. Must land decently."

Rosamund looked eagerly through the crowd to the group of competitors at the head of the slope. Would Otto von Vierling be there, she wondered. During the last week she had caught only fleeting glimpses of him. It was no good denying it, in spite of all that had happened, she wanted to meet him again. She knew quite well why the last few days had seemed faintly unsatisfactory. How could anything be enjoyed to the full if one was constantly hoping for the arrival of one special person?

Her eyes travelled swiftly from one to another of the group. They rested on one particular man who was kneeling down, adjusting a ski. He rose. There was something familiar about the figure and her heart leapt. It was Otto von Vierling, smoothing back his fair mane with one hand while with the other he pointed out some object in the valley.

There was a sudden movement among the spectators, a quickening of interest. Some vanished from sight and reappeared a few moments later on the flat ground at the foot of the run. Some pressed closer to the jump itself. A young Swiss, with a No. 1 emblazoned across him, took up his position at the start.

He was off.

A murmur of admiration rose as he flew down the slope and took off from the platform. With arms whirling to preserve his balance, his skis took the snow again far down the second slope. A second murmur—this time of commiseration rose as at the final turn he slipped and sprawled in the snow.

"Rotten luck," murmured Will. "But, gosh, what a jump!"

An instant later No. 2 was loosed like an arrow down that terrible slope. The jump was less spectacular but the finish was neat and well under control and won cries of "Bravo, Bravo!"

One after another, the dark arrows shot downwards, leaving the earth in their stupendous leaps.

At last the fair head swung round and Otto von Vierling glided into position. No. 8. Rosamund watched him make some joke as he handed his ski-sticks to an official.

"He's a dead cert for it," predicted a man on Will's right. "No one can touch him for style."

He was off.

There was a dead silence as he shot out into the air. A roar of applause greeted his return to earth, several feet ahead of No. 1's jump, the longest so far. The roar turned to a murmur of consternation as Otto crashed headlong into the snow, rolling over and over till he reached the soft snow to one side.

"Never seen him muff before," murmured the man on the right. "Wonder if the feller's hurt?"

Otto was examining one ski that had come loose, pointing it out to the men round him. He was helped off the track, waving his hand and smiling in acknowledgment of the chorus of sympathy.

There was only one more competitor, and then each was to have a second and third trial, but Rosamund looked in vain for Otto. He made no further attempt.

It was over. She persuaded Will to climb to a little hut a short way above them, where they could sit on the bench that surrounded it and eat their picnic lunch in the bright sun.

It was an ideal spot. The hotel lay far below them, a child's toy building, the ice-rink peopled with little darting ants. The valley on either side

of the promontory on which Reinigen was built
lay still and white and peaceful. The Enghorn,
angular and dark, defied the snow to lie on the
face of its dark cliffs, though its sisters, the
Wildberg and the Litzhorn lay meekly enough
in their white cloaks. The chain of white peaks
stretched in a semi-circle round them, while
behind them tier upon tier of snowy slopes hid
the farther ranges from sight.

"Isn't it too heavenly!" murmured Rosamund.
"I can't imagine why this gorgeous hot sun
doesn't melt the snow. I do hope Otto von Vierling wasn't badly hurt," she added irrelevantly.

"Couldn't have been," said Will. "Otherwise
he wouldn't be coming up here now. Good lord,
don't jump so! You nearly upset my lemonade."

Rosamund had turned with a start to face the
path.

Otto von Vierling was coming towards them,
in skis once more, though treading warily.

"You have a knack of choosing very delightful
spots to rest, Miss Rosamund," he smiled. "May
I join you again?"

Will stared from one to the other. Rosamund
had never confided either the incident on the boat
or her mistake on the nursery slopes. Mechanically
she introduced Will and inquired after Otto's leg.
He assured them that it was nothing more than
a slight wrench, but that as there was a championship race coming off at the end of the week, he
had been advised to jump no more.

Now that Rosamund was face to face with him
again, all her embarrassment returned. The more

she tried to appear at ease, the more difficult it became. She, to whom words usually came so easily, found herself tongue-tied. Luckily, Will kept the ball rolling by asking endless questions on jumping to which Otto replied with great good humour.

Otto had unfolded his lunch and was obviously about to partake of it with them. Rosamund wondered frantically whether she should refer to her mistake on the slopes? She was in such a turmoil of doubt that even Will noticed her silence, and inquired whether she was feeling all right.

Otto turned to survey her for a moment, then bent over his lunch. He tore a small piece of white paper from an envelope and stuck a match through it. He laid a sandwich on a bed of grease-proof paper and planted the improvised white flag in it.

"Will you have a ham sandwich, Miss Rosamund?" he asked. His eyes were twinkling as he held out the peace offering, but there was no mockery in them, only the bond of a joke once shared.

The relief to Rosamund was enormous. He knew the worst and yet was prepared to seek her out and hoist the flag of peace.

"I should love one," she said happily.

"I say, what nationality are you?" asked Will in his direct fashion.

Otto laughed.

"I begin to wonder myself," he admitted. "English, Danish, Austrian, but mostly English."

"You speak it perfectly," said Rosamund.

"I should do, for I've spent most of my life over there," he replied. "My mother was English, you see. My father was Danish."

"But Vierling isn't a Danish name, surely?" asked Will.

"No. I have only recently taken the name of von Vierling." Otto answered. "Oh, it's a very long and boring family history. I wouldn't dream of inflicting it on you."

"Please do!" cried Rosamund. "I love family histories."

Otto hesitated.

"Well, if you really want me to, I'll tell you the story. It's all concerning my great-grandmother. She and my great-grandfather were Austrian. She really is a wonderful old lady. She's over ninety-five now. I have been spending these last few days with her. She lives by herself, away over the mountains there." Otto waved his hand towards the snowy heights behind them. "She has lived there fifty years and more. It's a sort of self-imposed exile. My great-grandfather was once adviser-in-chief to the Grand Duke. That must be nearly seventy years ago. But unfortunately he was accused of some intrigue and was banished from the court. It must have been a put-up show for it nearly broke the poor man's heart. I have seen one or two of his letters written during his exile. Even then he can't bring himself to speak harshly of the Emperor. He lays the blame on certain of the courtiers who were jealous of his friendship with the Grand Duke.

Well, he made a home of sorts in Denmark, where my grandmother and her brothers and sisters grew up. But soon afterwards he died, and as her daughters were by this time married—my grandmother married a Dane—and her sons out in the world, my great-grandmother chose to retire to Switzerland, where she has lived ever since."

"But what made you change your name?" asked Will.

"I'm just coming to that," said Otto. "It appears that there was a lawsuit that dragged on for years concerning the property that my great-grandfather had to abandon in Austria. For when the Emperor died, a pardon was granted to my family and a restitution of all their land. This in the meantime had been sold, and what with the legal fees due to the years it has taken the family to establish the claim, I imagine that most of the fortune has been eaten away. However, my great-grandmother has still a considerable amount of money, and she wishes me to inherit this. But she made one condition, that I should change my name to my great-grandfather's, Otto von Vierling. She is the Gräfin von Vierling."

"Did all this happen when you were a child?" asked Rosamund, who had found this a story after her own heart.

"Great heavens, no!" cried Otto. "This only happened about three months ago. I went up to Oxford last term as John Hansen and the same term I came down as Otto von Vierling. It was a most curious feeling, as though I myself might change personality. Mother didn't like it at all. She's very—British. But she knew my father would have wished it. He was killed in the war. He went over to Denmark to help prisoners to escape. The Germans found him . . ."

Otto paused.

"How rotten," murmured Will.

"We used to come here sometimes in the holidays to see my great-grandmother," went on Otto. "She never seems to change. She's now just what I remember as a little boy, only the chalet and the mountains and old Fritz and Anna have shrunk a little. Fritz was her page boy about seventy years ago. She still calls him 'der Junge.'"

"It must be terribly lonely up there," said Rosamund. "Does she have lots of visitors?"

Otto shook his head.

"No one comes now," he said. "Her children are all dead and her grandchildren scattered all over the world. She never asks after them. She lives in a world of her own. I think that the day my great-grandfather was exiled and dishonoured, something broke in her as it did in him. She lives over and over again her girlhood at the Austrian Court. The years between mean nothing to her. When she sent for me last summer, she seemed quite surprised. I think she still expected me to be the six-year child I was when I first saw her. But she was quite lucid over her wish for me to change my name. What an interminable amount of legal business it took too! It even got into the newspapers—to my mother's horror."

"How pleased the Gräfin must be to have you here," said Rosamund.

"I suppose so," said Otto slowly. "But I think we of the present are only shadows to her. The past is more real to her than any of us. She has even forgotten her life in Denmark. It has been like that for years, Fritz told me. Poor woman, she lost her sons when they were quite young too, and I think that may have told on her mind. But somehow with it all she remains a very . . . great lady."

"How strange it all sounds," mused Rosamund. "John Hansen, Otto von Vierling, all one person."

"I wonder whether they are." Otto's eyes were fixed gravely on the mountains. "I can almost feel them as two separate beings. I had always thought of myself as English, my father was employed in an English firm, my mother was the daughter of an English clergyman. But when I leave England and think of myself as Otto von Vierling, I find I am really happier speaking French or German—we spent a lot of my childhood abroad. There is nothing in the least mysterious about John Hansen, but strange things happen to Otto von Vierling, unaccountable things."

He spoke with a curious intensity that made Rosamund and Will turn to him.

"Such as?" asked Will.

Otto was laughing again.

"I shall soon grow superstitious up here in the mountains," he said. "What will John Hansen think of me? The truth is, I have a strange misgiving that someone, some spirit of the mountains wishes poor Otto ill."

"What do you mean?" cried Rosamund.

Otto swung round and looked from one to the other of them.

"Can you tell me why the screws were loose on my skis to-day?" he asked. "I might have broken a leg on that jump, if not my neck. Why were they loose when only last night I tightened them with my own hands?"

A faint chill wind floated across the valley. The three were silent.

"I expect some ass mistook your skis for his and messed about with them in the store-room last night," suggested Will.

"Is there a big enough ass to take several screws out of these clips and replace them with ones of the same size head but far shorter, so that the change would be unnoticeable until a strain jerked them out?"

Again there was silence. Rosamund shivered. Almost, in that roof-top of snow, she could believe in lurking spirits who grudged human intruders. But her common sense quickly assured her that no mountain sprite would dabble in such a means of vanquishing a foe, with every elemental means of avalanche and boulder at his disposal. There must be an explanation. Perhaps the old man in charge of the ski store had tried to be helpful. Her mind turned once more to the old Gräfin in her chalet in the mountains.

"How I should love to meet your great-grandmother," she said aloud.

Otto ate the remainder of his biscuit and cheese before replying.

"How good are you on skis?" he asked.

"Not very," she confessed. "I'm better than I was, but I can't do all the turns like Will. He's frightfully good already."

"Rot," said Will modestly.

"I should very much like to take you over to the chalet," said Otto thoughtfully. "I go over myself every day. Fritz seems to think that something is on my great-grandmother's mind, something that keeps troubling her. I'm always hoping she will tell me what it is. Anyway, I'm sure it would please her to see one or two visitors. The point is this. It's a good five miles from here, up hill and down dale, and no road near it is passable in the winter. You'd have to ski there."

"I expect I could manage it if you'll be kind and not go too fast," said Rosamund gallantly. "But it would be rather a bore for you. You'd better just take Will."

"Nonsense. I'd like to take you," repeated Otto. "I tell you what. We'll go down now on to the nursery slopes. I won't do any ski-ing to-day, but I might be able to teach you a few things and I can see if you'll be able to make the journey or not."

Poor Rosamund! The next hour was a bitter one. Otto stood on the slopes, shouting directions, sending her back again and again to practise her turns, till her knees ached and her heart felt like bursting. He never seemed satisfied but was intent on further and further improvement.

W.H.   E

At last Rosamund dragged herself gasping up to him.

"It's no good," she said, almost in tears. "I'll never be good enough."

Otto saw her distress and caught her by both hands.

"My dear girl, you were grand!" he cried. "D'you think I should have taken all that trouble with you if you hadn't been so promising? What a brute I am! I oughtn't to have kept you at it so long. Look, I'll take you on a trial run to-morrow, and the day after, we'll make the big trek. How's that? By George, look at Will! That christie was first-class. He has the makings of a fine ski-er. Now, how about some tea? Can I join you?"

Rosamund gladly agreed, explaining on their way back to the hotel, all about Mrs. Vandermeyer and the impossible Lewis. He agreed to join what Rosamund called the Loo-is Mission and threw back his head in laughter at her stories of their efforts.

As they mounted the hotel steps, Rosamund paused.

"Do you honestly think that someone tampered with your skis on purpose?" she asked suddenly.

Otto halted.

Will, who had caught them up, halted also, to wait for Otto's answer.

"If that was all, I should never have given it another thought," he said slowly. "As you suggested, I should have put it down to some good-natured meddler. But there's something else, although that's probably entirely my imagination. You see, ever since I left London, I think I have been followed."

"Followed!"

Will's amazed ejaculation seemed quite inadequate compared with the sudden panic that gripped Rosamund. Followed! Otto had spoken the words quite calmly. Yet something sinister was taking place, here in this land of pleasure and fun. Something sinister. A pair of white hands flashed through her mind, hands that gripped a newspaper, eyes that for once had shown keen interest.

She caught Otto by the coat sleeve.

"I know who is following you," she heard herself whisper.

It was Otto's turn to be amazed. He swung round, his face incredulous. "What on earth do you mean?" he asked almost angrily.

Rosamund's confidence oozed through her feet into the doormat. "I don't really know," she stammered. "I just thought the little dark man . . ."

Otto gave a short laugh.

"So you just thought the little dark man . . . did you?" he said. "Congratulations, Miss Sherlock Holmes. I'm sorry. You rather took me by surprise. Actually, you're perfectly right. Our chase started from a second taxi that had driven up opposite to our house, just when I was leaving to come here. I caught a glimpse of him then. My destination was easy. My luggage was plastered with hotel labels. I must have given him a nasty fright when I left the train at Berne, but I suppose those labels had convinced him I should turn up here before long."

"Otto, how can you be so calm about it?" gasped Rosamund. "Oh, don't you think you ought to go to the police?"

"What on earth would that chap want to follow you for?" put in Will.

"That time alone will show," said Otto lightly. "But that he is after Otto von Vierling and not John Hansen, of that I'm convinced. By the way, don't show any special interest in him. It's most important that he shouldn't know I've spotted him. When did that friend of his turn up? Lugubrious-looking fellow with those great tea-saucer black eyes."

"He was here the night of the dance," said Rosamund. "I noticed him and the way that they were watching you in the hall."

Otto thought for a moment, then with a sudden change of mood, flung open the door of the lounge.

"We're being absurd!" he cried. Rosamund, don't look so worried on my account! Who's to say that the little dark man doesn't lodge in a house near ours and that the gods of chance haven't brought him along here to play in the sun of Reinigen?"

Rosamund tried to join in Otto's mood of gaiety, but the strange chill was still on her. How curious that those white hands should from the first have seemed so sinister to her. It was all so unreal. How could any one wish ill of Otto, with his gay, whimsical face and his charm and courtesy? Could the old lady, astute in her twisted mind, have turned a private detective on to watch Otto's movements, to see that he was worthy to inherit her wealth?

"A penny for them?" asked Otto, watching her thoughtful face.

"I was thinking of you," said Rosamund simply, only to flush hotly at Will's amused grin.

But Otto did not laugh.

"Thank you," he said. "I may need friends like you and Will one day. This following business might conceivably get on one's nerves."

That evening the majority of the hotel had emptied itself out on to the skating rink. Arc-lights were trained on to the ice while Japanese lanterns floated apparently in mid-air between them. The band from within was relayed through amplifiers to the accompaniment of the grinding scratch of skates.

Rosamund remained on the edge of the rink, content with the rhythm and the brilliance of the spectacle. A professional skater in ballet dress now held the centre of the rink, diving, gliding, twisting with exquisite grace and ease. There was a roar of applause as the vision vanished from the spotlight and couples swung out once more into a waltz.

It was at that moment Rosamund noticed that Lewis was standing beside her, muffled up to the ears in a purple scarf.

"Hallo! I didn't think you liked this sort of thing," she said.

"I don't," said Lewis uncompromisingly. "Ma sent me out. She's always telling me I don't act like you two. I'm about sick of it."

In spite of his rudeness, the boy looked so genuinely wretched that Rosamund decided the Mission must go on.

"You mean your mother wants you to go out and do more?" she encouraged. "You know, you'd be much happier if you did. You don't look as though you have much fun. Why don't you try?"

"Aw shucks, what's the good," said Lewis, turning on his heel and making for the darkness. Rosamund, hampered by her skates, could only make a grab at his arm.

"Do come back!" she begged. "Can't you tell me why you're always so unhappy?"

Lewis paused. For a moment he looked as though he would speak. But the Mission was foiled, for at that instant Will skated up to them.

"Come on, we're going to play Fox and Geese!" he shouted. "Gosh, haven't you got your skates on, Lewis?"

Muttering something inaudible, Lewis escaped from the detaining hand, and Rosmund was swept on to the rink to join the laughing gaggle of geese.

It was after a ten-step, the intricacies of which she had been trying to fathom, that Rosamund caught sight of Otto at the edge of the rink. He detached himself from a group of men to come over to her.

"I'll teach you the ten-step one day," he said.

"In the meantime aren't you getting frozen standing there watching? Do say yes! I can't skate with this ankle of mine and I'm trying to inveigle you back into the lounge to keep me company."

Rosamund looked doubtfully at Will, who was making a gallant attempt at the steps amid much laughter and good-natured teasing.

"No need to worry about Will," smiled Otto, following her gaze.

"Of course I'll come," said Rosamund. "I— I am rather cold."

"What a nice child you are!" nodded Otto. "You can tell me the story of your life. But before you begin, I must tell you something. I have had a note from old Fritz saying that he is seriously worried about my great-grandmother. This means I shall have to go over to-morrow morning. Now, how do you feel about it? Will you come?"

"But your ankle!" cried Rosamund.

"Nothing that a night's rest won't cure," he assured her. "How does that sofa suit you? Pleasant and undraughty. I like red plush. Very well, to-morrow we'll make it. Of course I can't promise that you will see my great-grandmother. She may be unwell. I really must try to get to the bottom of what's worrying her. Fritz told me she kept mentioning some jewels. I asked if there were any in the house, but he declares she has nothing but a diamond cross that she always wears. Fritz said, too, that she kept mentioning my name in connection with them, but as my name was also my great-grandfather's, old Fritzy may have got the wrong end of the stick."

"It's all so extraordinary," murmured Rosamund. "So extraordinary and so fascinating."

"I'm glad you're going to see her," said Otto. "I think she is unique. I can't imagine that she will ever change, ever die. Each year she may get a little smaller, a little more wrinkled, but she and her house and her old servants, they're as everlasting in my mind as the mountains behind the house. It's as though she had been—petrified, she can neither go backwards nor forwards in time. Dear, dear, I invite you to tell the story of your life and I do nothing but talk about myself and my affairs! The trouble is that you're too good a listener."

"I shall get you to put that down in writing!" laughed Rosamund. "I'm always being told that I talk too much myself."

She grew serious again.

"Otto," she said. "You must please be very careful, won't you? I'm quite positive that the little dark man is following you. Even in the train he frightened me. I hate his hands."

"Second sight, eh?" Otto laughed softly. "Very well, I'll be careful. I have my eyes wide open, I can assure you. For instance, follow the direction of my finger."

Rosamund glanced along the row of empty chairs. "I don't see . . ." she began.

"No?" Otto rose to his feet. Slowly he strolled towards the door, Rosamund obediently in his wake.

"Well, Miss Rosamund," he remarked. "I hope you won't be too stiff after that ski-ing practice this afternoon. It's tough on the muscles to start with."

For a moment his change in tone puzzled Rosamund. Then she noticed the deep plush chair by the door. Two white hands hung limply over the arms. They drew level with it. The dark man lay stretched out in the depths of it, his eyes closed, apparently fast asleep.

They crossed the hall to the lifts.

"I'm sorry our talk had to end," said Otto. "But I wanted to check up on that fellow. I saw him come in soon after we did. Actually you should try to get an early night. To-morrow will be more of a strain than you expect. Good-night—no, wait! I think we are about to act in a little comedy."

The small dark man had strolled yawning into the hall. He crossed to the lift with the intention of following Rosamund and Otto into it. But Otto stepped politely aside, as though he still had more to say to Rosamund. The man hesitated only for the fraction of a second, then stepped into the lift, waited an instant for them to join him, then closed the door. The lift bore him upwards.

"I expect he'll get out at the first floor. He can watch us from there," said Otto softly. "Strange, isn't it? Rather like becoming an actor in a crime play. Difficult for me to act convincingly when no one has taught me my part. Who has committed the crime, he or I? After a while, one begins to suspect every one and everything. I wonder what has happened to his singularly unattractive gentleman friend?"

There was a breath of icy air as Miss Drover marched into the hall, clad in a garment that resembled a hearthrug sewn up at the corners. She nodded pleasantly to the two.

"Wonderful sight out there!" she called. "Ready for bed to-night, by George! Glorious trudge. Right along the road to Bhul. Knees stiff. Not so young as I was."

Miss Drover always spoke as though despatching innumerable telegrams.

She pressed the bell for the lift, which as Otto had predicted, seemed to descend only from the next floor. Rosamund followed her, and, taking Otto's advice as to an early night, was soon in bed.

But tired as she was, she could not sleep. Long after the band had packed up and the shouts and laughter from the rink were silent, she lay thinking over the events of the day. Was Otto in danger? What could it all mean? Was it nothing but a series of coincidences? It was so easy to suspect every one and everything—coincidence. Of course it was coincidence. Coincidence. She repeated the word again and again to comfort the little sick feeling of apprehension that lay at her heart.

CHAPTER FIVE

THE GRÄFIN

WILL and Rosamund were both down early to breakfast. Otto strolled in a few moments later and joined their table, as Mrs. Vandermeyer breakfasted in her room, and Lewis scarcely ever made an appearance before ten o'clock.

The dining-room was deserted, but as they passed into the lounge they noticed the small dark man writing at one of the desks, a glass of orange juice beside him.

"Let's give him a run for his money," suggested Will. "Otto, you wave to us and go upstairs. I'll collect your skis. You can come down the fire-escape and give him the slip. Gosh, it sounds rummy, doesn't it? I still can't believe there's anything in it."

Otto shook his head emphatically.

"Presuming there is something in it, that would be bad policy," he said. "Above all things, I don't want him to know I suspect him. He's not to know that I spotted him inside that taxi. No, we'll saunter out under his nose. I shall be interested to see whether that will lure him out on to skis."

Accordingly they fetched their skis and fore-gathered outside the porch. Otto stooped to fasten Rosamund's skis for her.

"Has he moved?" he asked softly.

Rosamund glanced cautiously through the window.

"No. He doesn't seem a bit interested," she said.

"H'm," said Otto. "I wonder. I wonder whether he isn't interested because he is so sure of where we're going. Well, time alone will show. Ready, Will?"

It was a brilliant day. The sun had just made its way between the mountains, casting a million diamonds on the white ground. There had been a slight new fall during the night and the snow was perfection.

"Just like icing sugar," said Rosamund unromantically as they plodded up the first slope. "Did you ever smell anything so heavenly as the air? Only one more week of this. Oh dear!"

Otto had insisted on her leading the way so that she might set her own pace. He had provided her and Will with skins to tie on their skis, as the first hour of the journey was a steady climb.

At the end of a few moments, however, Otto called a halt.

"My dear girl, if you keep up that pace, I shall be having to carry you by the time we reach the top!" he laughed. "Slowly and steadily were your orders. I think I'd better lead. Call out when you want a rest."

The climb began again. Otto had been wise, for Rosamund found it comparatively easy to plod along in his tracks. Even so, she had little breath to spare, and they climbed in silence. It was a wearisome business. Desperately anxious not to be a drag on the others, Rosamund lost all count of time and distance, concentrating all her endeavour on the thrusting of one ski in front of the other, one after the other, on and on and on.

At last, after what had seemed hours to her, Otto again called a halt.

"Look!" he said.

They had reached a new view, hidden completely from the hotel by the long slope that they had just climbed. The slope had narrowed into a valley, where jagged hills rose steeply on either side. Only in one spot, far ahead, did the snow rise smoothly between those rocky cliffs. It was certainly a wild and lonely world that they had now entered. All ski-tracks had been obliterated by the snow the previous night. They might have been in the wilds of Tibet for all the sign of human life there was to be seen.

"This is the head of the Blumentaal, the Valley of Flowers," said Otto. "In the spring all this ground is a carpet of gentians. There's our path —between those two hills. Do you see it? Once up that, all will be easy. How do you feel? Can you go straight on?"

"Rather," said Will, whose lankiness had a surprising power of endurance. "I say, this is a wizard spot. Glad we haven't got to skip up to the top of those cliffs. That pass looks good fun. Forge ahead. I'm not a bit blown."

Poor Rosamund, whose ideas of bliss at that moment would have been to sink into a feather bed, turned again and obediently followed in Otto's footsteps. Again there was no sound but the sh-sh of the soft snow as they went up and ever up towards the cleft in that dark chair of rock above them.

It was over.

Gasping and triumphant, Rosamund leaned on her sticks to gaze over the new panorama that had enfolded before them. A fresh range of mountains tiered in the distance, separated from them by another valley. On the right, the slopes stretched more gently, following beneath the cliffs through which they had just passed.

"Take off your skins now," recommended Otto. "You'll find it a perfect run from here. Follow me exactly. Don't take any short cuts, Will. There are some pretty tricky places here and there. Eat some of this chocolate, Rosamund. You look a bit done in."

"Nonsense!" declared Rosamund indignantly, at the same time accepting the chocolate as a drowning man a straw, as it betokened an excuse for another moment's rest.

However, the next few minutes were sheer joy. Their way led down gently curving slopes, the snow spurting up behind them as they swept out of the blue shadow of the mountains into the clear sunshine beyond. Otto chose their path with great care, always selecting the easiest way, so that when at last they paused, it was to find that neither Rosamund nor Will had suffered more than one or two tumbles.

Joyfully Rosamund shook the snow out of her dark curls. "It was wonderful!" she cried. "I should like this to go on for hours. How much farther is it?"

Otto looked approvingly at her. "You did very well," he announced. "Now for a level bit. Then a short climb and one more run."

The climb was only the promised short one, and before many moments they found themselves on a pathway that wound gently downwards towards a knot of pine-trees. Among the pine-trees stood a chalet, itself of dark pine, with painted green shutters.

"Isn't it lovely!" breathed Rosamund. "Just like a toy one I had when I was little."

They had reached an open gate and a fence, whose wooden posts peered out of the snow. They followed the path past a row of wooden out-houses and cowsheds, their painted lofts laden with straw, till they came to the main door. The snow had drifted against it and lay untouched.

"We had better go round to the back door," said Otto. "You must forgive the state of things. Fritz and Anna are so old. In the winter none of the peasants will come up from the valley to work here. It's too remote."

They made their way round to a yard where an attempt had been made to clear the snow and free the doorway. Otto ushered them into a flagged kitchen, where an old woman, her legs encased in thick blue worsted stockings, her skirt tucked round her knees, sat in a chair engaged in plucking a chicken. At sight of Otto she threw up her hands and let forth a torrent of German, to which Otto laughingly responded. Smoothing her skirt over the expanse of red flannel petticoat, she clattered out of the kitchen, to return a moment later with her husband, Fritz.

Rosamund clutched Will's arm at the sight of Fritz. How much younger was Fritz than the Gräfin? It must be at least fifteen years. Yet Fritz looked so old that a breath might blow him away. He was a little man, grown smaller with age, a snow-white beard drooping on to his shiny black coat, and a pair of mild and faded blue eyes.

"Rip van Winkle himself," murmured Will.

Fritz had now embarked himself on a torrent of German, while Anna, with a great many clucking noises of concern at their being kept standing in the kitchen, led Rosamund and Will to the parlour.

The parlour was as much part of a bygone age as Fritz and the smiling Anna. Will's scant German had dried up completely before Anna's flow of apologies, as she shook the heavy chenille curtains, peeped into the china stove in the corner, patted the snow off Rosamund's coat and proffered Will slippers. But her goodwill and her expressive gestures were easy enough to understand, and she seemed quite content with their shy "danke-schön's."

They looked in delight at the patterned tiles of the stove, an immense edifice that towered to the ceiling. The room itself was of dark panelling, the chairs of heavy Victorian velvet, with the exception of a delicate Regency settee, its gilt now sombre as the rest of the room. By the stove stood a chair, long and straight-backed, covered by some patient hand in cross-stitch. Nearby was a little table with a few books and a bundle of grey knitting upon it. For the rest, the furniture was dark and heavily carved. A cabinet full of china stood stiffly by the door. A few ferns in pots of brass trailed their green leaves wearily over their wooden pedestals.

Rosamund sniffed appreciatively.

"Willie boy, isn't this thrilling?" she murmured. "Think of all the people who must have sat bolt upright in those chairs on their best behaviour sipping their tea. No, it was probably coffee. I suppose some of those lovely little cups out of the cabinet were used for special occasions. Look, that cross-stitch chair must be the Gräfin's. That little bead-work footstool was made to match it. And look at those lovely embroidered samplers on the wall! This one has got a name on it. Elsbeth von Arnheim.

"Aged eight years," translated Will. "I wonder if Elsbeth was the Gräfin as a girl? Do you think I could go and take a peek at those guns in the passage? They're absolutely super—ought to be in a museum. I'm jolly glad we came."

"I'm sure the whole house ought to be in a museum, Fritz and Anna included," said Rosamund. "Look at that little modelled shepherdess in the glass case. I'm sure all the china is simply priceless. I wish we could go and explore the rest of the house."

There were footsteps in the passage that heralded Fritz's arrival with a jug of steaming cocoa and some cakes.

"Vairy nice," he announced. "Vairy cold day. Vairy nice hot."

His English deserted him, but he stood silently beaming at them like an aimiable geni, his wispy white beard mingling with the white steam from the cocoa.

Gratefully the two accepted the striped blue jugs and fell to on the cakes.

They were soon joined by Otto.

"I just went up to see my great-grandmother," he said. "She struck me as being very weak. Anna tells me she keeps on mentioning this mysterious jewellery, but I can't make her speak of it now."

"Do you think Will and I ought to stay?" asked Rosamund. "I'm sure she won't want strangers."

Fritz, who had been trying to follow the conversation, seemed to catch the meaning of the last words. He nodded his head vehemently.

"Doch, doch! Visitors vairy gut. Die Gräfin like visitors vairy gut." This was followed by a volley of German at Otto in which Anna joined from the doorway.

Otto smiled at Rosamund.

"There's your answer," he said. "Fritz and Anna say that visitors do the Gräfin a power of good. They think it will take her mind off this curious obsession about the jewels. Anna says that she got up specially early to receive you. I sent word back to Fritz, you know, that you might be coming."

"Is this where she sits?" asked Will, pointing to the cross-stitch chair.

"She always sat there till about ten years ago," explained Otto. "Since then she has scarcely left her room, but Anna is always hoping that one day she will feel stronger, so she keeps this room dusted and ready for her."

Rosamund looked pityingly at the grey scarf that would never be finished and the sedate chair that would never hold its mistress again. Seventy years of exile! What did the Gräfin think of, all through those long days and months and years?

"If you've finished your cocoa, we'd better go up," said Otto.

"Otto! But I can't speak German!" cried Rosamund in sudden dismay.

"Don't worry," Otto reassured her. "Great-grandmamma speaks excellent English. Shall I lead the way?"

They followed Otto into the passage and across the hall, which was hung with hunting trophies of a century ago, and on, up the twisting wooden staircase. Their footsteps echoed on the uncarpeted floors, bringing a jarring note of life into the silent corridor beyond.

Otto knocked at a door at the far end of the corridor. A faint voice answered. He stood aside to allow Rosamund and Will to enter. After the darkness, the brilliant sunshine was dazzling. They saw that they were in a long, low-ceilinged room. An ancient carved bed stood at one end, while all the light of the room was concentrated on a small recess in the angle of the wall. There, before a row of windows fringed with spotless white net, stood an enormous chair. In the chair sat an old lady, her eyes fixed intently on them.

The Gräfin wore black, a stiff silk that enveloped her tiny figure. Her white hair was bound smoothly round her head and gathered into a little lace cap. Her hands were folded in her lap. Her face was very white, a network of tiny wrinkles, still showing, however, the delicate bonework that must once have been great beauty. She sat as still as the chair itself. Only her eyes moved questioningly from one to another of the young people. A diamond cross glittered from the lace at her neck.

"Here we are, dear," said Otto, bending over her chair. "This is the English lady I told you of, Miss Burnaby. This is her brother, Mr. Will Burnaby."

One of the thin hands moved and was held towards Rosamund and then to Will. There was something royal in the gesture. Will, with sudden genius, stooped and kissed her hand. It was certainly the correct procedure, for the Gräfin nodded approvingly at the brother and sister, then folded her hands once more. Even that slight effort seemed almost to drain her of vitality.

"I think this place is very beautiful," ventured Rosamund. "We have never been to Switzerland before."

"Austria is a very beautiful country," said the

tired voice. "The Emperor's palace is very great and famous. I must take you over it. My husband is the dear friend of the Grand Duke. Will you be here to-night to attend our dinner? We have seventy guests and there will be dancing in the ballroom. If you will excuse me, I must make my preparations. Call my page-boy, Fritz. He has to fetch my ball-dress from the dressmaker. He is a good boy, Fritz. He will make a fine servant when he is older. He has a loyal heart. It is a great thing to have a loyal heart."

The voice trailed off, and the poor tired eyes closed. They had seemed her one window of life, and the little figure now sat as still as though life had already fled. There was something inde-scribably pathetic in listening to that voice. To what bygone dinner had she invited them, wondered Rosamund. It was like stepping back seventy years of time, with Fritz's white beard as testimony to the missing years.

Her eyes turned to Otto, who leaned against the window. He had been right. The three of them were only shadows in this room. Age dwelt there, age in the panelled walls, age in the twisted carving of the dressing-table where the silver mirrors and brushes gleamed from the darkness. Age clung in the stiff folds of brocade that hung from the bed. Above all, age hovered over that chair, over that slight shadow of human life, awaiting the call to the court of the Greatest Emperor of all.

All at once Rosamund noticed that the dark eyes were fixed on her.

"Are you Otto's affianced?" asked the Gräfin.
Rosamund flushed scarlet. "No," she said.

Help came from an unexpected quarter.

"My sister is too young to contemplate marriage," said Will, with a fine attempt at court language.

"So? I was married at sixteen. My Otto gave me this diamond cross. I have worn it all my life. The others I would never wear. I feared them."

"What others, dear?" asked Otto quickly. "Other jewels?"

"There were six hundred at the reception. It was at the castle, for the Grand Duke loved Otto dearly. He drank to our health. 'To my well-beloved Otto and his wife, the Rose of Vienna.' It was such a beautiful day. I remember the flowers. The lilacs were still blooming when we returned from our honeymoon. There was a little summer-house by the lake. It was my joy to sit there. Otto knew always where to find me. Otto and I, we loved each other and we were happy."

Again the tired eyes shut and the flicker of life seemed to be spent. Otto bent over her chair, a deep pity in his eyes.

"Shall we go, liebe?" he asked softly. "Have we tired you?"

The Gräfin looked up at him. She pulled his hand down to hers and held it between her frail fingers. "No, no, you cannot go," she said, a sudden urgency in her voice. "I have something to tell you. I must tell you."

Her voice faded and she looked up at him in bewilderment.

"Otto!" she said, her voice quite changed. "I do not wish you to ride to-night. Stay with me!"

She clasped Otto's fingers imploringly.

"I will stay, dear," said Otto soothingly. "I will stay with you."

She gave a little sigh and lay once more with closed eyes.

"She thinks I am my grandfather," murmured Otto. "He was killed riding home from Great-grandmamma's to his home. He had only been married a few months. It was after his death that she came to live here."

"What did you say?" The old voice spoke again, but again with a new tone. The Gräfin looked from Otto to the others.

"I do not know who you are," she said plaintively. "Do you go to the ball at the palace to-night? They are lighting the gardens with coloured lanterns and the river will be illuminated. It will be a great spectacle."

Like a tide, the past washed over her.

"Otto, it was the fault of my greed," she sighed. "Yet I never wore them. I went against his wish. I disobeyed him. I am so troubled." She clutched his arm. "Have I told you what troubled me?"

Otto leaned over her, his arm round the trembling shoulders.

"No, dear. Please try to tell me."

She searched his face as though to clear her own poor mind.

"I had visitors," she said suddenly. "Such a

pleasure. We talked of old times. It was the son of the Graf von Eldheim and a friend. His father knew my Otto so well. He was like his father. His face at once was familiar to me. Such a great pleasure it gave me."

"I'm sure it did," murmured Otto. "Now I am going to take these visitors downstairs and give them lunch. Shall I send Anna to you?"

The Gräfin nodded silently, her eyes closed. Rosamund and Will followed Otto to the door, which he shut behind them.

They made their way down to the dining-room, a room packed tightly with heavy Victorian furniture and hangings. Otto, having despatched Anna to her mistress, took his place at the table with them.

They ate their soup in silence, too stirred by the memory of that quiet room upstairs to break it. Only as Fritz came to clear their plates did Otto speak, to give him a brief description of the Gräfin's state. One remark of Otto's caused old Fritz to gesticulate wildly.

"Doch, doch, ist wahr!" he protested.

"What was true?" asked Will, whose German had allowed him to grasp Fritz's last remark.

Otto turned a puzzled face to them.

"You know Great-grandmamma mentioned two visitors?" he said. "Fritz says it's perfectly true. They came the day before yesterday, two elderly gentlemen. One was the son of the Graf from Eldheim, who Fritz says was a very great friend of my great-grandfather's. Fritz knew the family well by name, though he was too young to remember the Graf. He said that the Gräfin was so happy to see them. They talked of the old days, and although she was exhausted afterwards, Fritz says that she laughed and chatted with them as though she was quite strong again. I wonder how they came to hear that she lived here? Fritz didn't know that, but no doubt they were on a tour and heard her name mentioned in one of the villages. Every one knows about her in the valley. Very plucky of the old fellows, wasn't it? It's no mean climb up from the village, and Eldheim must be pretty elderly himself."

"Do visitors often come here?" asked Rosamund.

"Very rarely. At first—yes. But gradually all her generation have died and the younger ones have forgotten her. Occasionally a friend turns up—like these two—whose parents knew her. But most of them are now pretty old. Look here, it's past two o'clock. I'm going to take you home soon. The run back is nothing compared with the climb up the Blumenthal, but I don't want you benighted. Have a doze while I run up and see if there is anything else I can do for Great-grandmamma. I offered to stay here in the house, but Fritz thinks it unnecessary. It might even upset her. Anything unusual upsets her, and no one has slept in this house but herself and Fritz and Anna for fifty years. Try that chair by the stove, Rosamund. I shan't be long."

Rosamund rather thankfully accepted Otto's suggestion, while Will elected to examine the ancient rifles in the passage. She stretched herself out in the chair and tried to picture in her mind the scene in that strange bedroom upstairs. But the picture faded into nothingness.

She woke to find Otto looking down at her. His eyes were curiously bright and restless.

"I haven't been asleep!" protested Rosamund. "At least—oh dear, I think I must have been!"

"I think you must too!" smiled Otto. "I've been waiting for you to wake up. Rosamund, listen carefully to what I have to say. Tell me at the end whether the same thought strikes you that has struck me."

Rosamund was wide awake now.

"I have been talking to Great-grandmamma again. She was quite clear in her mind and told me to wish you good-bye. She then began to talk of these visitors. It was delightful to see the pleasure they had given her, and it appears that they have promised to come again, possibly next week. I thought while she was in this mood I'd try to find out what has been troubling her. But it was no use. Fritz bears out that when she's in these lucid moods, whatever it is doesn't seem to trouble her. It's only when her mind is wandering. But, Rosamund, listen to this. Just as I was going, she spoke again of the Graf von Eldheim. She said how like his father he must be, for the face was familiar at once. Then she added, ' I do not remember the name of his friend with the long nose.'"

"Ye gods!" Will had joined them. He stood wide-eyed with excitement.

"You think what I think?" asked Otto sharply. "Bah! It's impossible. Why shouldn't the

Graf have a long-nosed friend? But just for one moment it struck me that the two visitors might turn out to be our friends from the hotel."

"You mean the dark chappie might be impersonating the Graf?" asked Will. "But the Gräfin couldn't be mistaken over a face. She said she recognised him. Well, if he's genuine, our little dark chappie is the genuine Graf. Not my idea of a Graf, I must say. More like three-pen'orth of lace over the counter."

Otto shook his head.

"No, I think this is another coincidence. After all, long noses are common enough in all conscience. Besides, Fritz said both these men were elderly and grey-headed."

"Just another coincidence," said Rosamund doubtfully. "Otto, we can't go on explaining things away by coincidences! We simply must check up on all these people. Let's start on it the moment we get back from the hotel."

Otto shrugged his shoulders.

"I told you what it would be like," he said. "Once having started these suspicions, we fall on everything that happens and attribute some dark motive to it. Come on. We must get booted and spurred."

Fritz, with infinite labour, had been clearing the snow so that they could make a grand exit through the front door. They tore themselves away from the pleasant smell of baking that came from the kitchen, and set out into the cold of the afternoon air.

As Otto had promised, the return journey was

a far less strenuous affair. The sun had moved
so that it fell now on the valley below and lighted
up the rocky heights above them.

"Now you can see the Blauer Gletscher," said
Otto, pointing to a sea of snow. "The peak above
it is the Teufelspitz. It's a great deal higher than
it looks from here. In the summer you can cross
over the Blue Glacier. There's a pass beyond it
that is the shortest way down to Interbhul. But
don't imagine I'm taking you that way to-night!
There's a crevasse there that's not safe to cross
even in winter. The locals won't go near the
place. They say the whole mountain belongs to
the devil. They swear that he blows hot air up
through the crevasse so that he can always pass
through it into the world. It's obvious how that
superstition came into being. There must be
some underground air current through the
crevasse for you can almost always see snow blowing up round it."

"I can't see the glacier or the crevasse," said
Will, shading his eyes and staring upwards.

"You can't see them at this time of year,"
explained Otto. "They're under the snow there,
up above those great cliffs. Even the guides
never go near if they can help it, partly superstition, partly the sheer danger of it. Come on.
It'll be dark if we don't hurry."

Once over the pass into the Blumenthal, the
going was simple enough. Otto shepherded them
down the valley, where the hotel lay like a doll's
house below them, the first lights of the evening
twinkling from its windows. The nursery slopes

hove into view and the familiar little world of
Reinigen closed round them once more.

At Otto's orders, Rosamund and Will betook
themselves upstairs to soak in steaming hot baths
to ward off the otherwise inevitable stiffness.
When they returned to the lounge for tea, Otto
was not to be seen. Mrs. Vandermeyer and Lewis,
however, were seated there, and for once Mrs.
Vandermeyer's cheerful face was scarlet with
annoyance. Lewis sat opposite her, ferociously
dismembering a cake.

Rosamund's heart sank. They had obviously
interrupted another family row, if anything so
one-sided as Lewis's growlings could be classed
as such.

Mrs. Vandermeyer made no attempt to ask
after their day.

"It's too bad," she began. "I don't know what
to do about Loo-is. I take him all over Europe.
I ask young friends out to keep him company. He
should have the loveliest manners, and look what
he does."

Mrs. Vandermeyer's fat face crumpled up with
misery.

"Aw, Ma, must we have all that over again?"
Lewis looked about as amiable as a trapped rat.

"He's been vurry rude," went on the outraged
Mrs. Vandermeyer. "Miss Fox-Strangways gave
me a book of her poems to read. Such beautiful
thoughts—all about sunsets and the evening of
life. Vurry vurry beautiful. Loo-is read one of
them and then laughed right in her face. She
just walked away. I've never felt so hu-miliated

in my life. Was it that you'd a headache, honey?" she asked suddenly, hoping at this eleventh hour to find some excuse for her darling.

"What's a woman like her want to write for anyway?" demanded Lewis. "That wasn't poetry. It was just a lot of silly old rhymes."

Faced with an unrepentent Lewis. Mrs. Vandermeyer looked helplessly at Rosamund. She drew her away from the table.

"You talk to him, honey!" she begged. "I think I feel my palpitations coming on. I'll just go and lie down a while. I'm positive Loo-is wasn't feeling too good this afternoon," she murmured as she turned to the door, a pathetic and disconsolate figure for all her rope of pearls and inexhaustable cheque-book.

When Rosamund returned to the table, Lewis had vanished. Will was eating his tea, quite unruffled by the storm.

"Our Mission doesn't seem to have got very far," sighed Rosamund. "Whatever is wrong with Lewis? I suppose he's gone off now in a sulk."

"He's gone to apologise to Miss Fox-Strangways," announced Will, buttering another roll.

"Will! However did you manage it?" gasped Rosamund.

"Told him I'd knock him down if he didn't," answered Will calmly. "I say, can we get some of this cherry jam to take home? It's super stuff."

CHAPTER SIX

SUCCESS OF A MISSION

IT WAS not for another half-hour that Otto made his appearance and demanded tea from the long-suffering waiter. He looked well pleased over something.

"I regret to inform you," he began solemnly, "that I have been guilty of gross defamation of character. First, I have been closeted with our Herr Proprietor, and secondly, I have been putting through a phone call to Berne. I am afraid our grand drama, our crime de luxe, our scintillating detective story—is dead. The little dark man is innocent. His friend is above suspicion. Coincidence has made fools of us."

He threw back his head and laughed.

"The ridiculous thing is that I now feel quite thwarted," he went on. "I had grown quite used to imagining myself the victim of an international gang. Poor Rosamund, you need never dream of white hands again. I've no doubt that Herr Brüne —that's his name—is an old-maidish bachelor who prides himself upon them. No, Will, no more giving any one the slip. How dull life will become! John Hansen has come to life again. Otto is altogether too imaginative."

In spite of his gay talk, Rosamund could detect the immense relief in him.

"Do tell us what you found out!" she cried. "How can you be so sure?"

"Right. I went and smoked a cigarette with Mein Herr. We discussed the international situation. We discussed chamois. We discussed the hotel business. Finally, we discussed the guests in the hotel. I inquired the nationality of the small dark man and his still darker long-nosed friend. Herr Geitzler knew them at once from my description. The friend is an Italian of the name of Mazzini. He keeps a curio shop in Berne. He is a great enthusiast and very knowledgeable and apparently many distinguished people patronise his shop. He left Italy for political reasons some years ago. Herr Brüne—now mark this carefully—is an Austrian whose business it is to travel round Europe collecting curios which he then sells to various dealers. Mazzini told Geitzler that Brüne had often done business for him and that they had met here for a few days to discuss further purchases and to talk over Herr Brüne's recent trip to London. So you see, apart no doubt from a little smuggling through the Customs and no doubt also a good deal of sharp practice over the buying of these curios, Brüne is as pure as the snow on the Jungfrau. No Eldheim incognito. That had been one of my theories."

"But why should he have been outside your house?" argued Will. "Can you explain that? Do you come under the heading of a curio?"

"There you get the most amazing coincidence of all," said Otto. "I realised it the moment I knew Brüne's profession. There is a large and very expensive curio shop just opposite my mother's flat. No doubt he had just bought or sold something."

"That doesn't explain why he took such an interest in you," persisted Will. "You said he was staring out of the taxi like nobody's business."

"That's simple too," said Otto. "As he walked from the shop to his taxi, he must have seen my suitcases piled on the seat by the driver. They were plastered in Grand Hotel luggage labels. Imagine the man's surprise at seeing my destination was the same as his! It must have struck him as a pretty odd coincidence. Naturally he was human enough to look and see who was stepping into the taxi, and naturally he was polite enough to draw in his head when he saw I was looking."

"Good lord, it all fits as pretty as you please," admitted Will. "Well, I suppose that's that."

"Any doubts left?" Otto turned to Rosamund. She shook her head slowly.

"It's lovely to think it was all a mare's nest," she said. "But I've still got a funny creeping in my bones. Perhaps it's only some more snow coming. That's what happens to Mrs. Elking, our cook."

"Gosh, what is all that chair-shifting in the ballroom for?" demanded Will.

"Progressive games, I think," said Rosamund. "Colonel Parker was talking about it yesterday."

Otto jumped to his feet.

"Come along, we must support that excellent

man!" he cried. "How about a little canvassing? There's Herr Schlacht. Herr Doktor, come and join us in the progressive games."

"Pro-gress-ive games? Vot is dat, Miss Rose?" smiled the professor from his chair in their neighbourhood. "I haf been play Breedge. Pouf! He is so hot in the Breedge-room. Do you not fint ze Switz hotels vairy hot? I am tolt all English like his hice colt."

There was a bewildered silence.

"Yes, ice is very cold," murmured Rosamund.

The worthy man slapped his knee. "No, no, I do not say dat!" he cried. "De hice . . . One house, two hice, is it not so? One mouse, two mice. I learn it at school."

Rosamund dissolved into laughter in which the good-natured professor joined.

"What a difficult language English must be!" she said. "No, we just say ' houses ' not ' hice.' Will you be my partner in the progressive games?"

"I am in your hants, Miss Rose," he said with a gallant bow. "As you say in English, ve vill stink or swim togethair."

The shout of laughter that greeted this remark brought Miss Drover and Miss Fox-Strangways to their table.

"Progressive games?" barked Miss Drover. "Splendid. Hope no nonsense like sitting on balloons. Here comes Mr. Ivor. Sit down quick, Jane. Pretend you're reading. Man's a public menace. Had the complete seven-volume novel of his phlebitis before tea."

The entire table became absorbed in picture

papers until the menace had passed by, his eager little eyes searching for another listener.

"Think we'd better start a daily hotel bulletin," suggested Miss Drover. "News of the day in brief: 11 a.m.—Mr. Brett has been seen to descend one hundred yards of the nursery slopes without falling down; 2 p.m.—Herr Doktor Schlacht has found a rare fossil in the foundations of the hotel. He is about to pull down the building to extract it; 3 p.m.—Mr. Ivor is found to be suffering from panjandrums of the silliphibia; 4 p.m.— Herr Otto von Vierling has bought another trunk to accommodate his thirty new challenge cups; 6 p.m.—Miss Drover is idiot enough to have promised to play progressive games. Something like that, what?"

They adjourned to the ballroom, where Colonel Parker was directing the setting up of the games. In twos and threes, barring the hardy perennials in the Bridge-room, most of the inmates of the hotel were gathering, some with the intention of playing, some merely to watch and jeer. Little did these latter know their colonel. Before they knew their fate, one and all were drafted to tables, while the Colonel himself outflanked those who attempted escape into the lounge.

Otto was in high spirits, and much was the laughter from the table where he and Miss Drover were engaged in picking up pins with scissors with which they were then inserted into small portions of slippery soap. Herr Schlacht was engrossed in the adding up of sums, in which he very shortly outstripped Rosamund, while Will and Miss Fox-Strangways were occupied in the highly intellectual pursuit of making faces at each other to see who would laugh first.

At the end of two minutes, Colonel Parker blew his whistle and half his regiment moved forward, their opponents in the opposite direction. Even the unwilling members who had been press-ganged into playing, were soon enjoying themselves and quite absorbed in the picking up of peas on straws or lighting innumerable candles.

It was at this table of candles that Rosamund, to her infinite surprise, came upon Lewis.

"Good gracious, I didn't expect to see you!" she said rather tactlessly. "I mean . . . You don't usually seem to care for this sort of thing."

"I don't," said Lewis. "Colonel Parker got hold of me. I was in the writing-room. Why can't the old devil leave people alone?"

"You're a little beast to talk like that!" cried Rosamund indignantly. "Colonel Parker's a marvellous person. Look how every one's enjoying this. Come on. There's the bell. See how many times you can light and blow out your candle before the bell goes again. Put a tick on the paper each time you blow it out. Then you count up the ticks at the end."

Purposely Rosamund did not try to make much speed, watching Lewis's clumsy and half-hearted attempts. Even so, she had succeeded in collecting almost double the number of ticks before the whistle blew.

"Thirty-eight," she announced. "How many have you?"

"Forty-two," drawled Lewis.

Rosamund looked contemptuously at him. What was the use of arguing? As they rose to change tables, she turned to him. "I shouldn't cheat at all the tables," she remarked icily. "Someone may turn nasty, someone who thinks you're worth bothering about."

It was a childishly unpleasant remark, and Rosamund's better self regretted it the instant she had spoken. But the result of her remark was most unexpected. Lewis, with a queer sort of gasping sob, stumbled out of the room.

Rosamund stood for an instant undecided, then hurried over to Colonel Parker.

"Will it upset the tables if I stop playing?" she asked. "Lewis Vandermeyer isn't feeling well and I think I ought to go to him."

She looked sadly at the next table where she and Otto would have met. But her better self was still in charge and a moment later she stood in the deserted lounge, wondering where Lewis had fled. She decided to try the writing-room.

She glanced through the glass doors. At first the room appeared empty. Then she saw a familiar head bent over the end desk. She walked quietly towards him and seated herself at the desk facing him.

The head moved and she met Lewis's eyes. He lowered his head instantly, but the sight of his swollen eyes was enough for Rosamund, who had always championed those in distress. Lewis being rude and objectionable was one thing, Lewis in tears was quite another.

"Lewis, I've come to say I'm sorry."

There was a muffled sob.

"It was a beastly thing to say. I'm so ashamed. Will you forgive me?"

There was a pause. Then the head was raised again. Lewis looked at her suspiciously.

"Did Ma tell you to come and jaw me?" he asked sullenly.

"Don't be ridiculous. I've not seen her since tea. I tell you, I came to say I was sorry."

"You needn't have bothered. I'm not worth bothering about. You were right. I cheated. I always do."

"Lewis, why? Can you tell me?"

"Ma always asks how I've done. If I lose, then she says I've got a headache. She won't allow I'm a duffer at anything. She tells every one I'm the cat's whiskers and then they snigger at each other because they see I'm rotten at everything."

He gave a jerk of his arm that scattered some papers on the floor. Rosamund stooped to pick them up for him, but as she did so Lewis sprang like a panther on them, hiding them fiercely under his hands. But he was too late. To Rosamund's amazement, she had seen pages of verse written in Lewis's spikey writing. New hope dawned like the rising sun. Perhaps she had at last found a fresh approach.

"I often write poetry," she said casually. "It's not very good I'm afraid, but it's a wonderful way of expressing one's feelings, isn't it? Is that your own verse?"

For a breathless moment she thought that Lewis

would retire again into his shell. As it was, he looked hard at her, then lifted his hand from the pages.

"Gee, you write too?" Her white lie was justified by the sudden eagerness in the boy's eye. "Can I see your stuff? What do you do?"

"I'm afraid I've nothing here to show you," said Rosamund truthfully. "But I'd love to read something of yours."

Lewis's pale cheeks were glowing.

"I'll let you see my last thing," he said. "It's a narrative poem about a whaler that gets ice-bound. They starve to death in the end."

Rosamund repressed a faint smile. Somehow she couldn't imagine Lewis's heroes with a happy ending.

"I mean to be well-known one day," confided Lewis.

Rosamund weighed her words.

"I doubt if you will be that," she said slowly. "You see, a true poet has a great soul. He has to have sympathy with other people. All the great poets have been men with loving . . . and . . . and kind personalities. You seem to hate everybody and it will show in your poetry."

"All poets suffer and are misunderstood," said Lewis firmly.

"Rubbish," said Rosamund. "They may suffer a bit from the—er—beauty of their feelings, but they don't misunderstand other people. They throw themselves heart and soul into life so that they can . . . can . . . throb with life . . . er . . . pulsate with the emotions of ordinary people."

Rosamund paused, having found herself in deeper water than she could manage. However, her words were having a visible effect on Lewis.

"Try to throw yourself into the . . . the maelstrom of life," went on Rosamund heroically. "Why don't you try here and now in the hotel? Come ski-ing with us and experience life . . . and . . . and speed and all that sort of thing. I guarantee you'll write better than you've written before."

"It might be worth trying," said Lewis. "But don't go telling Ma about the poetry! She'd have it all published in gold leaf before the day was out. How I hate all our money! I'd rather be down and out tramping the streets of New York."

"You wouldn't really. It would be abominably uncomfortable," said Rosamund firmly. "You ought to be glad to have so much money. Think of all the things you could do with it. You could found a rest-room for poor authors and poets or something. Oh, there are such millions of things that are possible with money! But just to please me, try what it's like to mix more with people. Give a little of yourself to others. They'll return it with so much added. You'll be much the richer and your poems will be the . . . the . . . the voice of humanity."

"Oh dear, I sound just like To-day's Bright Thought in the Sunday papers!" she sighed to herself. "Thank heavens Will isn't here. He'd tease me for evermore." She waited patiently while Lewis fiddled with the pens in the tray.

"I'll try," he said briefly.

"And Lewis," said Rosamund. "Do you think you could pop in and say something to your mother? She does love you so. I've always wanted to write a poem about a son who had been out years in the world and comes home to find his mother waiting just as he'd left her."

"Yeah, then they could all be drowned in a storm," said Lewis, so cheerfully that Rosamund had to let this wholesale slaughter go unchallenged. "I say, wait a bit. I'll go fetch that poem. I'd like your opinion on it."

Away he sped, leaving Rosamund to meditate on the gullibility of the male sex in general and Lewis in particular, and also on their glorious egotism, for Lewis was quite unaware of the sacrifice she had made on his behalf, or of the wistful ear she had turned to the distant laughter from the ballroom. However, she felt as some general might, who had fought a campaign over barren land, only to find victory was his by a detour through a green and fertile valley.

She snatched a piece of paper and began to write.

Miss Rosamund Burnaby to Mrs. Burnaby,
5 Beck Street, Hampstead, N.W.3.

Grand Hotel,
Reinigen, *Jan. 9th*

DARLING MUMMY,

Only one day since I wrote, but so many extra-ordinary things have been happening that it seems more like a month! We went for our first really long ski trip to-day, over the hills and far away, to see Otto von Vierling's great-grand-mother, who is an Austrian countess and nearly 100! It would take so long to tell you all about her that I'll have to wait till I get home. I'm so sleepy and my mind is such a jumble of impressions that I can't sort them out yet. I should be telling you that the Teufelspitz had snow-white hair and a lace cap and that the Gräfin wore a blue glacier! I've got another very long and funny story to tell you when I see you. I know you'll just say, 'Rose, what *will* you be imagining next?' But it wasn't only me. It was Otto and Will as well and we were all convinced that there were two crooks in the hotel. I was so proud of having spotted one in the train on the way here, and now we've found out that he's only a sort of high-class commercial traveller! It all sounds silly now but you've no idea how scare-making it was at the time! There, I hope I've told you enough to whet your curiosity nicely.

What I really want to tell you about is Lewis. Mum, I've done it! Believe it or not, Loo-is is a poet and he's promised to try to be a little ray of sunshine in future so as to enlarge his poetic soul! It's a shame to laugh at him as he's frightfully in earnest. Just as I thought, poor Mrs. Vandermeyer is half the trouble. It's a sort of vicious circle. Because Lewis behaves so abominably, Mrs. V. goes round telling every one how marvellous he is. And the more she talks like that, the more self-conscious Loo-is gets, and he goes on biting people's heads off because he thinks they're laughing at him. If only he can stick to it and be a bit pleasanter, I'm sure Mrs. V. will stop telling every one how wonderful he is. I'm sure she only does it to convince herself that he isn't quite as awful as he seems! How I hope it succeeds. I shall really feel I've repaid all her kindness—and she *has* been kind. I never knew any one so good-natured.

I can see Lewis coming in with his poems for me to read. I'll finish this later.

Later. Oh dear, I feel I've been through a hedge backwards. Actually I've been through about fifty icebergs and fifty days of starvation and am stranded on Greenland's icy mountains with Loo-is's whalers! It's a narrative poem about a whaling ship that founders. Of course, bits are frightfully funny, but there's a lot of imagination behind it. Perhaps I've ruined a genius by trying to turn Loo-is into a reasonable human being! I must copy you out a sample.

Starlight descending, ravenous, unhungry,
Beaten into pattern by thongs of knotted hands.
Primitive starvation, sunken eyes glowering,
into the acid water, hope, despair ravaging,
ravenous. Starlight descending, cloaked agony into
ravelled ecstasy of death impending.

Oh, Mum, they take eighteen pages to die! I didn't dare skip a word as Loo-is was watching me so anxiously all the time. I told him that I thought it was most unusual and he was delighted. He's a different person when he looks happy and excited.

I simply must stop. Will is playing progressive games but I expect he'll write to-morrow.

Your loving and very happy

ROSE.

PS.—Give Fuzz-Buzz a hug from me. I wonder whether she's like Lewis and was warped in her youth?

"Good lord, here you are!" said a voice.

With a start, Rosamund realised that she was still in the arm-chair in the writing-room. Too shy to join the others while the games were still in progress, and having finished her letter, she had waited there till she could tell Will of the success of the Lewis Mission. Lewis, fired with new inspiration, had abandoned her.

"D'you know it's nine and you've missed dinner?" demanded Will. "Thought you must have gone off to bed. You've hogged it for a couple of hours, young woman."

"How awful of me," apologised Rosamund. "Will, have you seen Lewis?"

Will looked suspiciously at her.

"I thought so," he remarked. "By some feminine and underhand wiles you've been straightening old Loo-is out. He said he'd been chatting to you. Chatting! Just been having a talk with him. Fellow was positively garrulous. What's more, I made one or two feeble cracks and Loo-is laughed! No kiddin', honey."

There was no one within earshot now, so hastily Rosamund told her story, which sent Will into guffaws of laughter.

"Wish I could have heard you at it," he remarked. "Mother V.'ll be like the cat with the canary. She had dinner upstairs, so she missed all the fun. Wonder if Lewis can keep it up? It's a jolly good show. Good-night, Herr Schlacht!"

The amiable professor turned to greet them.

"The snow is fall, you have seen?" he asked. "Let us hope it stop by morning. De snow on de ground is beautiful, but the snow when he falls is abominable. So I said to Herr Brüne when he leave."

"Herr Brüne has left, did you say?" asked Will.

The professor nodded.

"He go to Berne with Signor Mazzini."

Miss Drover had by this time joined them.

"Brüne? Brüne gone?" she demanded. "By George! Must see if I can snaffle his room. Proprietor said I could move there when Brüne left. Lovely room. Had it myself last year. Next to the bathroom at present. Sick to death of the filthy noisy waste-pipe. Nervous breakdown soon."

With a bark of laughter she vanished.

"So that's the end of Brüne," yawned Will as they reached their rooms. "Darned silly it all sounds now. Gosh, am I sleepy or am I?"

CHAPTER SEVEN

BEYOND COINCIDENCE

It was the afternoon of the following day.

Rosamund stood on the hotel steps earnestly watching Will's efforts to instruct Lewis in the gentle art of skating. With great unselfishness Will had decided that it would "boost" Lewis's morale to learn from someone so little better than himself. The reformation in Lewis still held, although lunch had admittedly been a difficult meal. Mrs. Vandermeyer had plainly been overcome by the miracle wrought in her son, but she had the good sense not to draw attention to it. Her eyes rested on Lewis in a dreadfully aggravating honey-I-sure-would-like-to-take-your-temperature-look. However, although Lewis wriggled uncomfortably under these looks, he remained adequately polite. He even admitted having enjoyed his morning on the nursery slopes.

Rosamund had a shrewd suspicion that the reformation was as much due to Will as to her. Will had taken no pains to hide his opinion about Lewis's manners to his mother and to the world in general, and she fancied that Lewis valued Will's opinions pretty highly.

She was soon joined by Otto.

"Are you and Will coming down with me to

the Championship Course?" he demanded. "I've promised to make a trial run down it this afternoon."

A wave of especial happiness passed through Rosamund. She was a modest and simple little person in spite of her exceptional prettiness, and it was still a source of wonder to her that Otto, whose friendship was so coveted in the hotel, should choose to spend his days in her and Will's company.

"Of course we'll come if we may bring Lewis too," she said. "You see, he might slip back so easily."

Otto, who had been kept up to date with every new phase of the reformation, smiled down at the earnest face.

"Very well," he said. "How about trying to reform me next? Which would you like to start on, John Hansen or Otto?"

"Oh, Otto . . ." began Rosamund. She flushed and faltered. She had been on the point of admitting that she could think of no faults in Otto to reform.

"Yes?" Otto waited in vain for her to finish. Then he gave a little laugh.

"You're so sweet, Rose," he said softly. "Don't ever alter."

With a sudden change of tone he added: "I say, let's call the others. I promised not to be late."

A few moments later saw Rosamund, Will and Lewis pushing their way along the path to the start of the course. Lewis had that morning, to the surprise of the others, admitted that he could ski to a certain extent and seemed glad enough to throw in his lot with theirs.

Otto had pressed ahead, as he did not wish to keep the committee waiting. He was still talking, however, to Colonel Parker when the others reached the spot.

They waited, not liking to join the group of gods of the ski-world, staring down at the slopes below. At intervals, small red flags marked the course. The flags led far down over another shoulder where they were lost to sight.

"I'll be up on the next funicular," called out Otto. "Who's below to time me?"

"Palmer and Johnson. They're waving now. Right you are. Go!"

The Colonel held out his stop-watch.

Otto pushed himself over the edge of the first slope.

"How easy it looks when you're as good as that!" sighed Rosamund, as Otto swung round in a spurt of snow to pass between the two first flags. "Where's the finish, Colonel Parker?"

"Over there." Colonel Parker pointed to the valley on the right.

"You can just see Major Palmer and Mr. Johnson. I doubt if von Vierling will take more than three minutes. It's a perfect run for an experienced ski-er. Flat out the whole way."

One of the committee moved over to them.

"Oughtn't von Vierling to be in sight now?" he asked.

The Colonel glanced at his watch.

"By George, yes. He's well over three minutes."

All eyes were fixed on the minute figures of the two timekeepers below. The stretch of snow before the final flags lay empty.

Four minutes passed, then five.

"Don't understand this," muttered the Colonel. "What's the fellow up to?"

They waited again. The men below were trying to signal some question. The minutes ticked on.

"Look here, I think we'd better go after him," said one young man. "He must have had a spill. May have lost a ski or something. Don't expect to see me yet awhile. I'm not out to break records. Whose coming with me?"

"Can I?" cried Will.

"O.K. Take it easy though."

Several members of the committee had already pushed off, Will manfully following in their wake in spite of all instructions.

"Don't look so worried, my dear," said the Colonel kindly to Rosamund. "Von Vierling will be all right. He must have met with some little trouble, that's all. I think he'd be very flattered to see your pretty face so pale on his account."

Lewis looked inquiringly at her but held his tongue.

Rosamund scarcely listened to the words. Ever since Otto's arrival had been overdue, she had been racked with a desperate anxiety. Some little trouble—like screws that didn't hold—some little trouble—some little trouble.

"Let's follow them down," she said at last. "I do so hate waiting."

Lewis's forehead wrinkled at the sight of the white abyss below them.

"Sorry. Can't take it," he said. "I can't stand heights. I'll never be any shakes as a ski-er. Say, what's happening now?"

The two timekeepers were climbing swiftly up and out of sight behind the shoulder.

"What the deuce!" cried Colonel Parker. "Something really must have happened to von Vierling! Wish to goodness I could get down there and find out."

"There they come!" shouted Lewis. "There's Otto! He's hurt."

"He can walk!" breathed Rosamund thankfully.

A knot of figures was making its way towards the funicular. In the centre was one figure, who apparently leaned heavily on the shoulder of another.

"Deuced bad luck von Vierling is having!" cried the Colonel. "He came a bad cropper jumping only the other day. Perhaps the same ankle is giving him trouble. Ah, now he's walking by himself. Can't be anything serious."

"Let's go to the station and wait for them there, Lewis," said Rosamund. "I must know what happened."

Once at the station, there was time to kill. Lewis, with surprising fineness of feeling, tried to distract Rosamund by talking of America and life in New York, showing a sense of humour and observation that would have delighted her, had she been able to give him her attention. But her whole heart and mind was concentrated on the funicular, that now loomed nearer and nearer as it rose towards them.

At last it came to rest against the platform and the compartments emptied. Rosamund picked her way over an old peasant, who was attempting to manœuvre a white goat away from a bale of straw, till she reached the door of the last carriage.

Several ski-ers had stepped out, and now turned back to give a hand to someone still within. It was Otto. He stepped out with a word of thanks, followed by Will. His forehead was plastered above the left eye.

"What happened?" cried Rosamund.

"A charming little practical joke," said one of the men. "Wait till I get my hands on the fellow that did it."

"Someone had moved the flags," explained Will. "They set them pointing right over a gully full of socking great spikey rocks."

"All's well that ends well," said Otto, as he moved stiffly up the steps. "It's all right, Rose. Come on, smile!" He looked down at the white little face beside him.

"Otto . . ." began Rosamund softly. "Do you think . . ."

"Hush! I don't know. Say nothing. There'll be a big shindy about this in any case."

The little cavalcade made its way back to the hotel. Otto, badly shaken, and with a deep cut on his forehead that had to be dealt with by the doctor, was soon the centre of an indignation meeting.

Colonel Parker strode up and down the lounge pulling at his moustache and breathing fire and slaughter. The younger men talked darkly of how they would deal with the practical joker, were he only to be found.

"I'd help 'em too!" snorted Miss Drover. "Criminal stupidity. Never heard anything like it. Moving flags bad enough. But to replace them *there*. Don't envy him when he shows up."

"They say Otto is only alife because he almost jomp the golf," added Herr Schlacht. "Any one else, he go ofer de bank and pouf! surely be kilt on the rocks."

Feeling surged even higher when it became clear that the culprit might never be found. The flags had been moved only a distance of about fifty yards, as the true course ran parallel to the gully. There were admittedly ski-marks, but as these only joined the innumerable tracks along the path in the valley, they led to no clue.

"You put the flags out yourself, didn't you, Palmer?" asked the Colonel.

The Major nodded.

"I did. But not till about two o'clock. We stayed down there and had a late lunch at the Belle Vue. We went back to the finishing post about three-fifteen, the time we had agreed on with von Vierling. The flags must have been shifted before we got back. You can't see that bit of the run from the finish."

"Must have been someone who knew nothing

about ski-ing," said another man. "No one in his senses would have left them there if he'd had time to think of the danger. I mean—well, dash it all—would he?"

"Supposing it wasn't a practical joke? Supposing whoever it was wanted to kill someone?" Rosamund's voice sounded shrill and unlike her own. She couldn't imagine what had prompted her to speak. Every eye was turned on her.

"My dear girl," smiled the Colonel. "Do you imagine that the hotel is full of homicidal maniacs? No, no. I agree that it was done by someone with very little knowledge of ski-ing, who never thought of the speed at which a first-class ski-er would pass between those flags. I very much doubt if it was done by any one in this hotel. More likely to have been a visitor to the Beau Site of the Belle Vue in the valley. My poor fellow, your luck has deserted you, von Vierling!"

Otto agreed politely to all that was said, but volunteered no fresh theory. At last he extricated himself from the swarm of eager avengers, and, making some excuse about letters, retired in the direction of the writing-room.

"Follow me in a minute," he murmured to Rosamund and Will as he passed by.

They accordingly waited until he had answered the inquiries which were fired at him from every chair in the lounge, then sauntered slowly after him.

Otto sat at one of the desks, staring ahead of him. The old line of strain had returned to his forehead and he looked utterly weary.

Will laid a hand on his arm.

" Look here, old man," he said earnestly. "You've got to do something about this. Let's tell the police."

Otto swung round on him.

"Tell the police what?" he demanded. "Just what have we to tell the police? Can't you picture their faces. They'd think I was crazy. Rosamund, Will, was the moving of those flags a joke? Or are we up against foul play? I've given up thinking. Funny, isn't it? If I knew for certain that someone wished me ill, I don't feel I should mind. But to have this happen when we had agreed that the rest was coincidence—I don't know what to think."

"Let's tell Lewis about it," said Rosamund suddenly. "He'll be thrilled to have a secret and he's a queer sort of boy. I believe he'd be very clear-headed over it. I should like to see how it would strike a complete outsider."

"You tell him," agreed Otto wearily. "My head isn't too good. You two can do the talking."

Rosamund persuaded Otto to rest in an armchair while Will sought for Lewis, who had rather sadly taken himself off to his room, abandoned as he thought by the others.

Rosamund's instinct had been right over Lewis. He sat enthralled while she and Will laid forth the story of the last week, while Otto threw in a word of explanation here and there.

When they had finished, he sat silent for some time.

"Whole thing sounds put up to me," he remarked at last. "You don't get chaps being such dawg-gone fools as to go moving flags for fun. They didn't even collar them for trophies. No. And you don't get them sticking them back in the one and only danger spot on the landscape. It ain't funny enough to amuse a grasshopper. They knew just what they were about, believe me. They must have got a motive for wanting you out of the way, Otto. What is it?"

"I can't imagine," said Otto. "I haven't an enemy in the world that I know of."

"Maybe. But aren't you mixed up in any one else's trouble?" persisted Lewis.

Will sprang to his feet.

"Otto!" he cried. "Someone else's trouble! That's it. What about your great-grandmother's jewels that she's ' troubled ' about?"

"I tell you they don't exist," said Otto. "Fritz would know of them, or Anna."

"Gee, Will's got something there," argued Lewis. "Supposing talk's got around about those jewels. It doesn't signify if they exist or not. It may be common talk in the villages that the old lady's got a packet tucked away somewhere."

"Then why on earth try to liquify me?" asked Otto.

"Haven't thought that one out yet," admitted Lewis. "Yeah, I've got it! They think the old lady's going to make her jewels over to you quick before they can lay hands on them."

"Pity if they despatch me for the sake of some jewels that don't exist," commented Otto. "Rosamund, don't look like that! They haven't got me yet. You may be right, Lewis. I mean to go over to the chalet in any case to-morrow. I'll try to find out if there could be any foundation to this story about the jewels. Great-grand-mamma may talk about them again herself. I particularly want to know if she has been talking about them to any one else."

"What about those visitors, Graf-von-how-do-you-do and his pal?" said Will. "Fritz said she talked a lot to them."

"After all," put in Rosamund, "he may be a genuine count, but that doesn't mean he's not a crook."

"I still don't see how he could have got here and changed the screws on my skis," mused Otto. "Still, it's a possibility. Perhaps I'll get to the bottom of it to-morrow. How about your all coming over with me? Do you think you could make the trip, Lewis?"

"We'll know by to-morrow evening," grinned Lewis. "Thanks a lot."

"Lovely," said Rosamund, who would cheer-fully have agreed to ski over the Sahara if Otto were to be of the party.

At that instant the hotel porter entered the writing-room. He came over to them and spoke rapidly in German to Otto. Otto nodded.

"Ich komme," he said, rising. He turned to the others.

"It seems I've got a friend waiting in the back quarters to see me," he said. "I wonder who the dickens that can be. Come with me if you like. It may be something of interest."

The three needed no second bidding. They followed Otto down the stairs and along the echoing stone passage of the basement. At a side entrance stood a Swiss peasant lad.

There was a quick exchange of questions and answers. Otto pressed some paper money into the boy's hand and he retired.

Otto looked extremely grave.

"That lad had a message from Fritz," he said. "The Gräfin is worse. Something—I don't know what—has happened to distress her. I'm going over there at once."

"Otto, you can't! Think of your head. And it's dark!" cried Rosamund. "Oh please, please be careful!"

Again the fear of the evil unknown filled her. It must have penetrated to the boys, for they scanned Otto's face anxiously.

"Can we come with you?" asked Will. "We might make ourselves useful some way."

"No, thanks." Otto shook his head. "I must make this trip as quickly as I can. Don't be hurt, old man, if I say I can go faster on my own. I shall have Karl for company."

"Are you sure he's—all right?" asked Rosamund. "He couldn't be . . . be one of them?"

"One of them," Otto repeated the words slowly. "Them. No, Rosamund, I know his face. I've seen him chopping wood for Fritz. Will, here's the key of my room. Be a good fellow and fetch my torch off the mantelpiece, will you, while I collect my skis."

"Are you sure you're fit to go? You look so tired." Rosamund was still deeply anxious.

"Needs must, my dear," he answered. "I tell you what. You three can still come over to-morrow if you like. I shall stay the night at the chalet, but I can send Karl to escort you over the Blumenthal Pass in the morning. He would be quite reliable as a guide. Funny. I had a feeling this might happen. I packed an emergency set of night gear in my haversack this morning."

Karl was recalled, and after a good deal of hammering of the plan into his wooden head, comprehension dawned on him, and he undertook to fetch the three at ten o'clock the next morning.

"Something's going to break, and break quickly," predicted Lewis, as they discussed the subject for the hundredth time on their way to bed. "Gee, I wish it was ten o'clock to-morrow!"

"D'you know, I'm beginning to like that chap a whole lot," said Will slowly as Lewis waved a brisk good-night.

CHAPTER EIGHT

ROOM 150

THE next morning, in their impatience to be gone, the three were ready long before the figure of Karl in his rough homespuns appeared on the scene. Will, in his best German, attempted to glean news of the Gräfin, but Karl merely grinned and thrust out his hands to express that he had not understood. After one or two efforts, Will gave up the attempt, and they proceeded slowly on their way.

Rosamund kept glancing back at Lewis. She wondered how he would stand the climb, for he was obviously in poor training. She paused tactfully every few minutes to admire the view.

However, in spite of this, Lewis's steps became more and more halting, and half-way up the Blumenthal, he sat down abruptly, his head between his knees.

"I can't—make it," he gasped. "Sorry. You'd better go on. I'm so darned giddy."

"That's only because you're not used to so much air in your lungs," said Rosamund kindly. "We're more than half-way up now. Do try. You'd hate to have to turn back now."

Karl had been watching this scene with interest. The truth seemed suddenly to dawn upon him, for, untying a long piece of rope from his waist, he knotted it round him, then handed the end to Lewis.

"He wants you to catch hold and pull," said Will. "Jolly good idea. It'll give you no end of a leg-up."

Rather shamefacedly, Lewis accepted the offer and their progress proceeded. Karl plodded steadily onwards, as though a mere cotton reel was attached to him, stopping to grin encouragement from time to time. Rosamund made the climb with less effort than before, though many were the moments when she would gladly have changed places with Lewis and his cord.

The pass was reached at last and the new world lay before them. No doubt with instructions from Otto, Karl cherished them down the slopes like an old sheep-dog, his eye ever on Lewis, who was the weak member of the party.

"There's the Blauer Gletscher!" shouted Will to Lewis, as they ski-ed under the shadow of the Teufelspitz. "They say old Nick walks around up there."

At his voice, Karl turned his head to look where Will pointed. A sudden expression of dread came over the stolid face. It was clear that the Blauer Gletscher held some superstitious terror for him, despite its spotless coating of snow.

The chalet stood in its screen of pines, as peacefully remote from the world as ever. There was not a sound, except for the soft clucking of Anna's hens in some barn. The front door was open, with Otto waiting there to welcome them.

"I'm so glad you've come," he said. "Great grandmamma is dying."

"I say, that's bad," said Lewis sympathetically.

"Oh, Otto, I'm so terribly sorry!" said Rosamund. "Have you got the doctor?"

"Yes. Come in and I'll tell you everything. So much has happened."

They handed their skis to old Fritz, who stood like a forlorn gnome behind Otto, his face more wrinkled than ever by grief. Old Anna peeped over the staircase, the tears rolling down her face.

Otto led them to the parlour. His face was pale, his eyes heavy from lack of sleep.

"I ought to have stayed here," he said with bitter self-reproach. "This need never have happened."

"When was she taken ill?" asked Will. "Was it a heart attack or what?"

"Sit down, all of you. I'll tell you the story from the beginning," said Otto. "It'll help me to clear my own mind. Well, I arrived here with Karl to find old Fritz and Anna almost beside themselves. It appears that Great-grandmamma was particularly well yesterday morning. Then, just before lunch, Graf von Eldheim and his friend turned up. Fritz went upstairs and asked whether she would like to see them. She was delighted. Fritz says that she even walked across the room to greet them. Fritz went down to the kitchen to tell Anna that the visitors would stay for lunch. He thinks he must have been down there about ten minutes, not more, when he

thought he'd better go back and offer the men
some beer. When he reached the stairs he heard
one of the men talking very loudly. He hurried
to the Gräfin's room, but von Eldheim's friend
stood in the doorway and wouldn't let him pass.
He slammed the door in his face. Poor old Fritz
was quite desperate. He could hear von Eldheim's
voice shouting angrily. There he was, alone in
the house but for Anna, no neighbours within
call, and as you can see, he's a very feeble old man
himself. He tried to hear what von Eldheim was
saying. He seemed to be questioning the Gräfin
about something, but Fritz couldn't hear any
words. He rushed down to tell Anna what was
happening. She, good woman that she is, seized
a red-hot poker out of the fire as a weapon.
There's no lock on Great-grandmamma's door,
and they had the sense to move very quietly. The
result was that they had the door open and were
into that room before the men could be on their
guard. Anna must have been a pretty terrifying
apparition. The Gräfin had fainted in her chair
and Anna at the time thought they had killed
her and was quite beside herself with fury. Anyway, she drove those two men out of the house
and, I imagine, gave them one or two pretty
nasty burns, as she says they departed cursing
and threatening to have the law on her. As soon
as they were gone, Fritz ran around locking up
all the doors and windows, and Anna went back
to Great-grandmamma. She had various remedies
and she managed to get Great-grandmamma
round from the heart attack that she'd had.

They got her to bed, and then luckily Karl was
due up with milk from the village, so Fritz sent
him straight off with that message for me. Poor
old Anna! When I arrived she didn't know
whether to be proud of having ousted those men
or frightened at having assaulted the aristocracy!
I assured her that no one would send her to gaol
and that I only wished she had roasted them in
her oven."

"Then the Graf and his pal are crooks!" gasped
Will. "They must be at the bottom of everything.
What do we do now? Ring the police?"

"Did the Gräfin say anything more to you?"
asked Rosamund.

"Otto, it *must* be the jewels that they're after!
Why are you so sure they don't exist?"

Otto turned gravely to her.

"I know now that they most certainly do exist,"
he said. "I sat up with her all night. Just as it
was beginning to get light, she became very quiet.
I felt she was saving her energy for some special
effort. Suddenly she said quite clearly in German:
'Otto, you must take the jewels. They are safe
no longer.' I just caught a few more words:
'Not here. In the mountains.' I went on questioning her very gently, but her mind was
wandering again and she thought I was one of
those foul men questioning her. She kept turning
her head from side to side and saying 'No, no,
they are for my Otto.' I had to give it up."

"In the mountains! That's a pretty tall order,"
murmured Will.

"Can't Fritz help in any way?" asked Lewis.

"No. He has never heard her mention them till just these last days. But when I questioned him closely, he said that he had a vague memory of a black box that the Gräfin kept in her room, years and years ago, when they first came here. He went to Austria to visit his relations soon after, and when he returned he noticed that the box had gone. He never thought of asking my great-grandmother about it. She never discussed her affairs even with Fritz. Well, to go on. I saw that everything was locked up, and early this morning I ski-ed down to the village to phone for a doctor. By an amazing piece of luck, I hit on a doctor from Musson, who was motoring through on his way to the T.B. clinic at Barg. He was a very decent fellow and came straight back with me. When we arrived, my great-grandmother had had another heart attack. He didn't mince words. He has promised to call in on his way back to-morrow, but he said frankly that it was only a question of days, perhaps hours. Nothing can be done. There's no question of getting in a nurse. She would far prefer Anna to look after her. Poor Great-grandmamma! I wish I had known her better. She bore misfortune with great dignity."

"Those brutes!" cried Rosamund. "They will be responsible for her death."

"No, not that," said Otto quietly. "The doctor said a shock might have hastened her death by a very little while, but as he put it, the sap has withered and the leaf must fall."

They were all silent with the awe of the young

who are faced for the first time with the greatest drama of life—death.

"Have you called the police?" asked Will.

"No," said Otto. "I didn't feel it—justified. What do we tell them? That old friends of the family stayed too long and caused an old lady to faint, and were then chased out of the house by an old woman with a red-hot poker? They would come in their hoards to the chalet. They would question old Fritz's word till he had contradicted himself fifty times. They would terrify Anna with their questions about burning the men with the poker. They would want to know whether the Gräfin wished von Eldheim charged with unlawful entry. They would even want to see her. No, it's impossible. I want tranquillity for her."

"If only we could fit all the bits together," groaned Will.

"Let's get Fritz to describe Eldheim and his pal again. We ought to make certain we can recognise them."

Fritz was called again into the room and made to recount the arrival of the visitors on both occasions, their looks, their clothes. The three others waited impatiently to hear the conversation translated.

At last Fritz could think of no more details, and he departed, more like a gnome than ever, shaking his head till his wispy beard floated round his shoulders.

"Good old man," murmured Otto, his eyes on the figure shuffling down the passage. "All his life given to Great-grandmamma's service. If it is in my power, I shall give the chalet to them for their own. Who has a better right to it than he and Anna? No, he had nothing fresh to tell us. As he said before, the one had a grey beard and almost snow-white hair. That was the count. The other was taller and grey-haired with a moustache. He could think of nothing remarkable about their clothes. He thinks one if not both wore glasses. It's not much to go on, but if we saw them together, they'd be easy enough to recognise."

"What are the chances they'll be around here again?" asked Lewis.

"Very small, I think," said Otto. "Anna is sure that they thought the Gräfin was dead. They're not to know that she rallied."

"Yes. But supposing they think the jewels are hidden in the chalet?" inquired Will.

"I still think they would be very unlikely to come back," said Otto. "If they think my great-grandmother died then, they will know that the chalet will have people in it, and it would be a great risk for them. I personally think that they'll now cut their losses and clear out. I shall, of course, take precautions, lock up the house very thoroughly at night and so forth. It's like a fortress with those heavy wooden shutters."

"Have you asked Anna what the men looked like?" asked Lewis. "Different people notice different things, you know."

Otto looked at Lewis with a sudden respect.

"You're right," he nodded. "I'll try her at once."

Anna, who had left her mistress asleep, was back in the kitchen, preparing lunch. She was quite willing to be questioned, though her voice rose in shrill anger at the mere mention of the men. As she detailed their clothes and appearance, Otto shook his head.

"Nothing new to add," he said to the others. "Except that she's sure both men were wearing glasses."

He turned, as Anna suddenly struck her hands together as though just having remembered something.

As Anna spoke, a look of utter amazement came over Otto's face. He questioned her swiftly again, to be answered by emphatic nods and assurances.

"What is she saying?" begged Rosamund. "Tell us quickly!"

Otto turned back slowly to them.

"Anna has just remembered something else," he said. "When she chased the men out of the house, von Eldheim was wearing no gloves. She noticed, because—his hands were so white and small—like a woman's."

For a moment they all stood as though turned to stone.

"Brüne!" gasped Will. "He and von Eldheim must be one and the same!"

Through Rosamund there passed a feeling almost of relief. So now there was no need to ponder on chance or the long arm of coincidence.

Her instinct had not misled her. The enemy was no longer in hiding. It was those white hands that tried to wreck their evil on Otto and the chalet.

"I suppose the other man was Mazzini," said Otto. "But there's still so much I can't follow. All that's clear is that somehow or other this man Brüne got to know of the jewels, and only recently, or he would have made this attempt before."

"But if Brüne is just Brüne, why did the Gräfin say he was so like the old Graf von Eldheim? And how did he know all the old friends that Fritz says he and the Gräfin talked about?"

"Yeah, that's a point," put in Lewis.

"Fritz didn't say that my great-grandmother recognised the Graf," mused Otto. "He used the same words as she used to me—that the Graf's face was familiar. That was all. But I think Brüne must in reality be von Eldheim, more shame to him. Otherwise, as you say, how could he have known all Great-grandmamma's friends?"

In spite of her grief and agitation, Anna before long produced a magnificent lunch. Otto scarcely touched any food, except when Fritz's eye was upon him.

As Fritz was clearing the plates, Anna's head appeared round the door and she spoke hurriedly to Otto. He rose at once.

"Great-grandmamma has just woken up," he said. "I must go up to her. Listen. If in half an hour, I have not come down, I want you to start back. I've told you I'm taking no chances. You're to get back to the hotel in broad daylight. I have already oiled Karl's grubby but reliable palm, and he will go with you."

"Oh, Otto, can't we stay?" implored Rosamund. "We might be useful. Do please let us stay!"

Otto hesitated.

"My dear, you know how I should love it," he said. "But Mrs. Vandermeyer would be frantic about Lewis—and I'd feel happier about you and Will."

"Why don't you let just me stay?" demanded Will. "Rose and Lewis will be safe as houses with old Karl. It won't be much fun for you here on your own, and I'd be handy if you had to make a sudden nab for the jewels."

"I wonder." Otto seemed greatly tempted. "I don't see why not. I might need to get a message down to the village for the doctor, or possibly the priest from Musson."

Rosamund and Lewis pleaded once more to remain, but Otto was adamant. He promised faithfully that Karl should be sent to escort them over again the next morning, and with that they had to be content.

The half-hour ticked slowly by.

There were no sounds from upstairs. At last, Fritz trotted into the parlour to announce Karl's arrival, and reluctantly Rosamund and Lewis prepared themselves for their journey.

In spite of Otto's precautions, it was all but dark before they reached the hotel, and Rosamund was thankful to retire to her room to rest.

It was a couple of hours later, when returning from her bath, that she cannoned into Miss Drover.

"Just moving house," announced Miss Drover. "Proprietor very decent about it. Pushing the next people into my room instead. Wish 'em joy of the waste-pipe! Surprising number of journeys moving your traps. Place looks like a jumble sale."

She looked disconsolately into her room, where clothes were strewn in heaps over the bed and chairs.

"I'll help you," volunteered Rosamund. "I've nothing special to do and there's heaps of time before dinner."

Accordingly she set to work to try to reassemble coats and skirts that were imprisoned under books and papers and to rescue Miss Drover's black lace frock from under her snow-boots.

Miss Drover returned from a trip to her new habitation.

"Hate clothes," she announced, looking admiringly at the order rapidly being restored. "Should like to wear a bearskin in the winter and a sheet in the summer. No trouble at all. Seen my hat? Funny. Don't know how the bed-leg got on top of it. Never mind. Seen better days anyway. D'you know, thought I was seeing things when I went into that other room just now. Switched on the light. Window was open. Opened it myself about an hour ago. Don't like other people's fug. There on the sill could have sworn I saw a hand. Thief climbing in. Looked round for something to hit him with. No fireplace, so no poker. Just going to take my shoe off when I saw it was gone. Must have been a trick of light, you know. Couldn't have been a hand, really."

"Why not?" asked Rosamund rather breath-lessly.

"I'll tell you why," said Miss Drover. "I say, be careful of that album. Rare pressed flowers, you know. I went to the window and looked out. Drop of thirty feet. Not a sign of any one.

"Weren't there any footmarks?" asked Rosa-mund.

"Several thousand. The room looks right over the drive."

Miss Drover pounced upon a collection of jumpers and dug her chin vice-like into the pile.

"Should have known it wasn't a real hand if I'd thought for a moment," she added. "Whoever heard of a burglar with white hands?"

Rosamund folded a skirt with trembling fingers.

"No. 150, is it?" she asked. "I'll take this lot along now."

She slipped into the corridor, her mind in a tumult. The white hands! No trick of light there. So Brüne—or rather von Eldheim—was back in the hotel. No. 150 had been his room. Why had he tried to get back to his room, secretly through the window? There was only one obvious explanation. He had left something behind, something worth the risk of discovery, something that could not be demanded of the hotel proprietor. The door of No. 150 stood open.

She laid the pile of clothes on the bed and then hurried over to the window, which Miss Drover had closed. With heart beating wildly, she undid the catch and leaned out.

All was quiet. Lights gleamed from between shutters. The hotel had gathered its inmates into its comfortable and solid care for the night. She looked down. There was certainly a drop of at least thirty feet to the drive. No man could have climbed up that smooth surface. There was not even a drainpipe to give any foothold. She looked to her left, where the long row of windows repeated themselves one after another, like objects diminishing in a looking-glass. There was a gap of at least twelve feet between this window and the next. She turned to the left, and almost immediately the explanation lay clear. No. 150 was the last room of the main block, adjoining the right wing, which was only two storeys high. To the right of the window, therefore, only some five feet away, lay the flat roof of the wing.

She leaned out as far as she dared. Yes. Brüne must somehow have made his way on to the roof, had managed to peer round the corner and grasp the sill. At that moment, no doubt the light had flashed on, he had withdrawn his hand and disappeared over the roof. But how had he known that Miss Drover would open her window? Had the catch been fastened, he could never have made his way in. Again the question answered itself. This was no premeditated crime. The man must have been lurking near the hotel, had seen the open window, and taken this unexpected chance. What did he want from No. 150?

She shut and bolted the windows, then feverishly began to search the room. The wardrobe was empty, the drawers were empty. She pulled back the mattress. In desperation she pulled out the dressing-table drawers till they lay heaped at her feet. She gave a sudden little cry. Behind the smallest right-hand drawer lay a small brown-paper packet. She snatched it up and thrust it into her pocket as Miss Drover came in, the pile of jumpers still in their vice.

"Good lord, child, no need to start spring-cleaning!" she exclaimed. "Now do run back and get dressed. Catch your death of cold in that kimono. Can manage quite nicely now. Very sweet of you to help. Ha! Nice to have a view to-morrow morning. Grease on that skirt? Bother! Must have been the skating boots. See you later."

Rosamund fled to her own room. The packet was not sealed. It was hard to undo the knots in the string, for her hands were trembling uncontrollably. There was tissue-paper inside the brown wrapping. In the tissue-paper lay an object that for a moment Rosamund was at a loss to understand. There was a quantity of black hair attached to a circle of parchment-like material. That it was some form of disguise was obvious. But what? The wig of a bald man with a beard to match? A very strange wig, with the exact circle of baldness at the back, of masterly workmanship, both it and the beard. It certainly was a most curious bald patch, almost like a priest's tonsure. She stood, frowning down at the hair, so horrible in its realism. A priest's tonsure. In a flash the thought came to her. This was a priest's disguise! There was the black beard that would hide Brüne's features. She pictured the robes and the flat clerical hat that must now be in Brüne's luggage. A priest! The only man who at this moment would have entrance to the Gräfin's room.

She pulled on a jumper and skirt for speed and thrust the packet into her pocket. She opened her door, but paused at the sound of voices coming down the corridor. There were two or three voices, Miss Drover's among them. Some instinct made her draw back and almost close the door.

The voices and footsteps came nearer. One man must be the proprietor.

"Nothing in the drawers yet," said Miss Drover. "You can turn them inside out as far as I'm concerned."

"Herr Brüne thinks his letters have got stuck maybe between two drawers," said the proprietor. "He was hoping to return to the same room, so that he need trouble no one."

"So I've done you out of your room, Herr Brüne? Beaten you to the post, eh?" Miss Drover spoke in that particular loud voice that the English so often use to foreigners. "Sorry, but you're only here for one night, didn't you say?"

"It is nothing, Madam. I return here from Berne for one day of happiness in beautiful Reinigen. I fetch my packet of letters and make it the excuse for a ski excursion to-morrow."

Rosamund could see nothing, but she knew

that the voice must belong to Brüne. The English was excellent, the voice quiet and respectful. She realised suddenly that this was the first time that any of them had heard his voice.

Breathlessly she waited till they had turned the corner of the corridor. She slipped out and sped in the opposite direction. Not daring to wait for the lift, she hurried down the stairs into the lounge. She must find Lewis.

Luckily Lewis was immersed in a detective story and had not yet gone up to change.

"Lewis, I want you!"

After one glance at Rosamund's face, Lewis was on his feet.

"Steady, honey," he said kindly. "What ghost have you been seeing?"

"Let's go down to the basement," she urged. "I want to go somewhere we can't be watched."

Lewis nodded assent and they strolled towards the staircase. Once down the stone stairs, Rosamund pulled Lewis towards the little empty hall where they had interviewed Karl the night before. Breathlessly she poured out her story.

"Don't you see, Lewis!" she cried. "They're sure to do something now. Mazzini may have another of these priest disguises. They may still try that. I don't see how they can suspect me of having . . . Oh, Lewis! Suppose Brüne finds the packet gone and asks Miss Drover if any one else has been in the room, and she tells him no one but me! He knows we're friends with Otto."

"H'm. Pity you didn't put it back," assented Lewis. "We don't want to put him on his guard."

"But if I'd left it, he'd have gone off to the chalet early to-morrow dressed up as a priest. It's the one disguise Otto and Will wouldn't suspect. He must have heard that the Gräfin was dying and that's why he wanted the disguise so badly."

"That's true enough," agreed Lewis. "Now what?"

"Lewis!" Rosamund clutched his arm. "We've got to get over there before them. We must go to-night!"

Lewis stared at her. "To-night? Are you crazy?" he asked.

"If you don't come with me, I shall go alone," said Rosamund defiantly. "Don't worry. I'll get there."

"But Rosamund," protested Lewis. "We're pretty dead beat and it's as dark as anything. We'd never make it."

"Of course it's dark now," said Rosamund impatiently. "But it won't be in a couple of hours. Don't you remember how absolutely brilliant the moon was last night We should see just as well as if it was daylight."

"I think we ought to get the police in," said Lewis. "I'd like to see Brüne under lock and key."

"You know Otto doesn't want the police called in!" said Rosamund reproachfully. "Anyway, Brüne would say the beard was for the fancy-dress ball. You needn't bother," she added. " After all, it's not the same for you. You haven't got a brother over at the chalet."

Lewis flushed.

"Don't be so darn silly, Rosamund," he muttered. "If you go, I go. But I tell you frankly, I'm not keen on it. If that Johnny suspects you've found his wig, he'll be watching you like a hawk. They may follow us."

"I've thought of that," said Rosamund. "I'm going to ask Miss Drover to take the packet along and say she found it among her clothes. She'll do it, I know. She's the sort of person who likes a bit of adventure and I'm sure she'd keep a secret."

"You've got something there!" said Lewis admiringly. "That should do it. Jehosophat! We'll give them a warm reception when they turn up to-morrow. Give us a look at the gear."

Rosamund carefully unfolded the packet and the two examined the amazing craftsmanship of the beard.

"I only hope I shall be able to make the packet look exactly the same as it did," she said anxiously. "Just two knots. I remember where they came and I can see where the paper was folded. Look. After dinner let's both say we're tired and want an early night. The moon should be perfect by about nine-thirty. We can send Karl over in the morning to tell your mother where we are. She never sees you before about eleven, does she? I don't want her to be worried."

"You've got it all buttoned up, haven't you?" Lewis looked at her with rueful admiration. "O.K. We'll meet down here at nine-thirty and collect skis, eh?"

"Right. You're an absolute brick, Lewis. Now for Miss Drover. I wish I knew where Brüne was at this minute. I don't want him to see me going to her room. Bother. I suppose we shall have to dress for dinner or it might look suspicious. We'll have to change back afterwards and then nip down the servants' stairs. It's no good hurrying too much. There's a good two hours before it'll be light enough."

They strolled slowly up towards the hall, Rosamund guiltily conscious of the bulge in her pocket. However, they met no one, and she was soon in her own room again, engaged in re-doing the packet to the best of her ability.

At last she was satisfied. She walked cautiously down the corridor to room 150, and knocked at the door.

Miss Drover, hair-brush in hand, listened silently to the strange request.

"Look here, Rosamund," she said bluntly, "I know there's something behind all this. I'll do it willingly—lie like a trooper if you want— always was inventive. But you're not getting into any sort of trouble here, are you?"

Miss Drover's keen eyes looked her up and down.

"No, no, it's quite all right," stammered Rosamund. "It's nothing really to do with me at all. It was just silly of me to take that packet when I knew it was Herr Brüne's. I don't know what possessed me."

"There, don't go wasting your fibs on me," said Miss Drover kindly. "Like to know the whole story one day. Never mind. Not your secret, I dare say. Always respect a confidence. I'll put the big deception over before dinner."

She looked up rather anxiously at the eager face beside her. "Don't go losing your head as well as your heart, m'dear," she smiled.

Blushing hotly to find that her feelings were so apparent, Rosamund murmured her thanks and slipped back to her room. She went through with the farce of changing into her white frock, and then descended as calmly as she could to the dining-room.

Mrs. Vandermeyer was all in favour of an early night for the two. They sipped their coffee in the lounge and then Lewis rose with a yawn.

"I'll be sleeping right away, so don't bother to come and say good night, Ma," he remarked. "So long, Rosamund. See you in the morning."

Mrs. Vandermeyer turned to Rosamund, her eyes filling as usual under the stress of any emotion.

"Rosamund, honey," she said. "I don't know what you've done to Loo-is, but he's a different boy. He doesn't get headaches or feel sick any more."

Rosamund couldn't help smiling at this euphemism.

"I don't know how to thank you and Will. It just isn't possible," went on Mrs. Vandermeyer. "You've given my Lewis something that money couldn't buy."

It was a pathetic little admission. Rosamund gripped her hand.

"I'm so glad," she said. "We're very fond of Lewis, Will and I. Now do you mind if I leave you? I'm terribly tired and I know you want to be off to your Bridge."

She bade her good night and slipped upstairs, wondering rather guiltily whether Mrs. Vander-meyer would have felt quite so grateful had she known on what hazards Rosamund was about to take her darling child.

She encountered no one. She fancied at dinner that she had seen Herr Brüne enter the room rather late. That Miss Drover had carried out her promise, she felt confident. Would Brüne notice the difference in the packet? Unlikely, for the folds were identical.

She changed into her ski suit, then lay down on her bed, her hands clasped behind her head, to wait for the moon. Once or twice she picked up her pen to attempt a letter home. Her library book was beside her. But it was hopeless to think of anything but that journey ahead of them. She must never let Lewis see that she was frightened, hopelessly, miserably frightened.

At last, between the pine-trees, rose the moon, full and golden. The moment had come.

CHAPTER NINE

JOURNEY BY MOONLIGHT

ROSAMUND pulled on her boots and added an extra sweater under her ski jacket. She hastily filled one pocket with chocolate and stowed her torch in the other. She unlatched the door and looked out. The passage was deserted and so were the back stairs. It was easy enough to reach the basement where the skis were stored. She retrieved hers from the stand and fastened on the skins. When she reached the back door, it was to find Lewis already waiting for her.

Poor Rosamund! It was one thing to make an expedition in the daylight, in a party where she was the one to be considered and cared for, but quite another to find herself the leader of the party, the party consisting of one ski-er, no better if as good as herself, by moonlight, and when both were already tired before they made the start.

"We've got hours to do it in," whispered Rosamund. "We must take it terribly slowly. We can follow this morning's tracks. Look, the moon will be shining right on to the Blumenthal. It ought to be quite easy to see."

"Not so funny when we're over the pass and the moon is the wrong side of the mountains," murmured Lewis.

"It'll be higher then. That's fine! We're on to the nursery slopes already."

They plodded on, trying to be content with their slow progress. Every now and then they turned back to scan the slopes below.

"We're not being followed, that's something," said Lewis. "We'll be right out of sight over that next ridge."

They followed the various ski-tracks up the Blumenthal, the rocky peaks at the valley's head cut clearly against the sky, like a backcloth to some vast stage. Here and there a light glowed from some peasant's cottage, but soon these were left behind, as they plodded wearily on, their eyes on the white stretch of the Pass. Had the one been fresh and the other exhausted, perhaps neither would have reached the end of the climb, for the one would have set too great a pace, or the other have been too dispirited. As it was, they achieved the climb, foot by foot, stopping to smile encouragement at each other, well aware that the other was in like condition.

"I didn't know knees could ache like this, did you?" sighed Rosamund. "I keep trying to think of vi-spring mattresses and bouncy sofas and lilos and deck-chairs and all the other lovely things I'd like to be sitting on."

"Doubt if I could sit!" groaned Lewis. "My ankles are going to disintegrate before long. I say, Rosamund . . ." His face looked very young and earnest in the moonlight. "D'you realise this is the first time I've ever done anything real in my life? Anything worth while, I mean, anything I wasn't just playing at."

Rosamund nodded sympathetically.

"I know, Lewis," she said. "You've been simply grand to-night. Look, we've only got that traverse to do and then we'll be up on the Pass. What's the time?"

"Nearly eleven. Gosh, we've taken two hours, double the time we took this morning."

"That doesn't matter. The light will be all the better on the other side. Come on."

Slowly they pursued the zigzag track of the morning up the Blumenthal Pass. The moon was lost to them here, but the starry sky was so brilliant that even in the shadow the tracks were visible enough. By sheer will-power, for they were both in a state of great exhaustion, they reached the Pass at last.

They paused on the summit to gaze in awe at the world beyond, remote and majestic in the cold moonlight.

"Come on, Lewis," gasped Rosamund. "I—I don't think I'll ever be able to go on again if I stop now. Sure your skis are all right? Whatever happens we mustn't twist an ankle or anything. Can you put my skins into your knapsack?"

Lewis's teeth were chattering with fatigue.

"Sure. Go ahead," he said. "Slow and steady—that's the motto."

To climb by moonlight had been comparatively simple, but it was quite another thing to attempt any speed down the slopes. The shadows played fantastic tricks that disguised distances, and the

angle of each slope was difficult to judge. Rosamund, however, had been right. The moon had
topped the shadow of the Blumenthal and now
lighted them on their way. They stuck rigidly
to the tracks of the morning, never venturing a
short cut, however tempting it appeared. Even
so, in their weariness and inexperience, falls
became more frequent, and to pick themselves up
more of an effort. Somehow they found that they
had reached the foot of the Teufelspitz, where the
Blauer Gletscher lay wrapped in shadow in the
folds of the mountain. By mutual consent, Rosamund and Lewis remained close to each other till
the shadow was passed. How easy it was to believe
the peasant stories of evil spirits, up there, in the
secret recesses of the moonlight.

Neither Rosamund nor Lewis could remember
how they accomplished the last mile or so to the
chalet. It was a blurred memory of aching limbs,
of innumerable falls, of a craving to lie down
and rest, even in the snow, anything to ease the
ache of weariness and cold.

It was after midnight before the two figures
staggered through the gateway of the chalet,
their eyes thankfully fixed on the lights from
behind the shuttered windows.

One window only was unshuttered. It was the
Gräfin's room. Otto stood at the window, a heavy
silver candlestick in one hand, his fair head
haloed in its light, his eyes far away, lost in
thought.

Suddenly his gaze fell on the two white, up-
turned faces below.

"It's all right.   Otto saw us," murmured Rosamund. "Everything's all . . . right . . . now."

The door was flung open. Hands reached out to draw them into the warmth. It was over, the nightmare ended, and she could rest.

"Otto, she's fainted' Is she all right?" Will's frightened voice came through the mists to her. With an effort she roused herself.

She was sitting in the kitchen. Will was holding hot soup to her mouth, while Anna chafed her hands and feet. Lewis sat opposite to her, his face thin and pinched in the glow of the fire.

Otto stood between them in great concern.

"Don't talk either of you till you're ready," he said gently.

"I'm O.K." Lewis drank off his mug of soup, while Fritz knelt down to unlace his boots. "Guess it's Rosamund's story, though. Something came through at the hotel and she said we'd best come over and tell you."

"My God!" Otto looked from one to the other of them. "You mean you've made this trip on your own?"

Lewis nodded. "Never want to see a darned mountain again," he said with a ghost of a grin.

Little by little their story was told. Otto and Will listened intently, Otto turning to translate now and then to Fritz and Anna.

"So you see, we had to come," said Rosamund simply.

"Why on earth didn't you tip one of the guides to bring a note?" cried Will, relieving his feelings in anger. "Plum crazy, both of you."

Lewis and Rosamund looked at each other.

"We never thought of that," admitted Rosamund weakly.

Otto took her hand in his.

"Thank you, my dear, for coming," he said. "And you, too, Lewis." There was a deep emotion behind the words. "And now, we'll sum up your theory. If Brüne suspects nothing, you think he will be up here as a priest, pretending he has heard of the Gräfin's illness. If, however, he is suspicious of you, we are to expect some other move to-morrow."

"Anyhow, you can count out the theory that they've packed up," said Lewis. "They're hot on the scent still. Make no mistake about that."

"How is the Gräfin?" asked Rosamund.

"Much the same," said Otto. "She has known none of us, not even Anna."

Anna had left them, to see to the preparing of another spare room for Rosamund. They sat and waited in silence, watching the blackened rafters where the bunches of herbs hung from the ceiling, and the flickering shadows cast by the big oil-lamp. Thoughts flickered through Rosamund's mind as the lamp shadows danced and fell. Idly she tried to think of a definition she had once heard of bliss. Bliss, the relief from pain. Then this was bliss, the warmth surging through her, dear Will's face, still glancing at her from time to time to reassure himself, Otto beside her, his eyes alight with that peculiar sweetness of expression that came at times to him, old Fritz, moving about in his carpet slippers, eager to be of service. It was a moment she would never forget, after the anguish and stress, to sit there surrounded by love and kindness, her hand in Otto's strong fingers.

Almost in a daze, she saw Anna beckoning at the door for Otto to follow her. She listened to the steady tick of the carved clock on the wall, backwards and forwards swung the pendulum, backwards and forwards, all a part of the blissful warmth that filled her.

Otto stood again in the doorway, and at his voice she was again wide awake. It held a new tone of urgency.

"The most extraordinary thing has happened," he said quickly. "Great-grandmamma has rallied. She is quite normal and herself. She asked if I were alone here, and I told her that all of you were with me. She seemed greatly relieved, for some reason, and said she wished to see you all. You, too, Lewis."

Rosamund rose stiffly.

"Of course we'll come," she said.

It was a solemn thought, to be visiting the room of a dying woman at midnight, yet all in keeping with the strangeness of the night. They followed the dancing light of the candlestick that Otto held above his head, till once more he opened the door at the end of the passage, and they passed softly in.

The room was lighted only by the two silver candlesticks on the dressing-table. A hundred tiny images stared back from the mirror at the bed where the Gräfin lay, her frilled lawn cap scarcely whiter than the face beneath it. Life still burned in the dark eyes that were fixed eagerly on the door.

"Come in," she commanded. "I wish you all close—so."

Her voice was surprisingly strong. She took Rosamund's hand in hers and motioned Otto to sit by her.

"Friends of my great-grandson's are friends of mine," she said graciously. "It is well you have come. So much has to be said, so much is there to be done. Otto will need help, your help."

Her eyes travelled over the young faces.

"We will help Otto, Gräfin," said Will quietly.

"So. Is good. I tell you everything. It is of the jewels, the emeralds the Grand Duke give me on my wedding day. No one was told of the gift. He feared the jealousy of others. The jewels were without price, a necklace and a bracelet. Perhaps he had no right to give them out of his family. Perhaps that is why they brought a curse upon us. They were so beautiful. I gaze at them for hour upon hour. Ach, Otto, I am a wicked woman!"

"No, no," said Otto, stroking her hand.

"It is true, Otto. I told a lie. I told it because I loved my Otto so much. When the Emperor listened to what they invent about him . . . when the Grand Duke banish him who was his best friend . . . Otto, my great-grandson, can you think, can you imagine how I feel? A man of his nobility and honour to have his loyalty questioned, to be turned from the court where he had been trusted. Can you imagine how I felt, I who loved him so? I was only a girl, laughing and playing with my children at my knee, but I grew old in that one day, for they broke my Otto's heart and all my love could not comfort him. ' Send back the emeralds,' he told me. ' I wish them to go back to the Grand Duke.' Otto, therein was my wickedness. I disobeyed him. I told him that I had given back the emeralds, but all the while I kept them locked in my room. It was my foolish stubbornness. I would not see Otto stripped of everything that had once been his. I thought, perhaps one day I sell them. I buy him a beautiful house and horses and the life he love. I waited always in great fear that the Grand Duke send for them. But he never did. I think his conscience was uneasy—he was a very, very proud man, else I think he ask my Otto to forgive him. He loved my Otto so. They had been boys together at the court. . . ."

Her voice ceased. Her eyes were fixed on the glimmering candles in the mirror, a faint smile on her lips.

The others waited anxiously, fearing that the past might capture her again. However, after a moment, she turned her eyes to Otto.

"The emeralds were useless to me. I could not wear them, I could not sell them for fear of questions. How could I tell my Otto that I lie to him, he who never in all his life have lie to any man. Always I comfort myself and say, one day we will need them. One day Otto will thank me for being wise. We will sell them for great

money and be happy ever more. One day I take
them out and I look at them and I clasp them
round my neck. They are so very beautiful. The
maid come into the room to say my Otto is taken
ill at the house of a friend. When I reach the
house of his friend, he is dead, my Otto. I make
a great promise that I now will do his wish and
send the jewels to the Grand Duke. But no, I
think. My sons may need the money. Why should
I give them back to him who took my Otto's
happiness from him? Once more I lock them in
my room. Soon after, I lose my dear son Heinrich,
the year after, my Kurt. I live now in Switzerland. I think I will rid myself of the jewels. But
no. I do not part with them. I take them far
away, but I still keep them. All these long years
I have kept them. They bring me ill-luck, for I
have the guilt of a lie upon me. But, when I am
dead, Otto, my great-grandson, they shall be
yours and they shall bring happiness and your
wife shall wear them like a princess."

"Where are they now?" asked Otto. "Would
you like to tell me?"

The Gräfin tried to raise herself, and Rosamund
put her arm behind the pillows.

"You must go find them, my child," she said.
"See. In my jewel-case is a lining of velvet.
Under the lining lies a paper. It is the Karte—
the map of the mountain. It shows the höhle
where they lie."

"What is a höhle?" whispered Lewis to Otto,
who had now opened the lid of the jewel-case on
the dressing-table.

"A cave." Otto's fingers lifted out the tray to search the faded well of velvet below. He crossed again to the bed and bent over the Gräfin.

"I have the map, Great-grandmamma," he said.

"You must . . . go . . . at once." The voice had sunk, the words scarcely audible. "Go . . . now."

The sudden surge of life had left her. Otto slipped his hand on to her wrist. After a moment, he nodded, laid the hand gently back on the cover, then beckoned to the others.

"She's not . . .?" whispered Will.

Otto shook his head.

"No, no. I can feel her pulse. We'll fetch Anna. I think she should have one of her capsules." They tiptoed from the room, each profoundly moved by the scene they had witnessed.

Once more in the kitchen, with Anna despatched to care for her mistress, the four leaned over the table in the arc of the lamplight.

Otto smoothed out the small piece of paper that had lain in its hiding-place for so many years. It was certainly a map, finely drawn, with here and there a distance marked or a peak shown. But although the drawing was painstaking enough, it was obviously not the work of a practised hand. There were no names written on it, no landmark such as the chalet itself.

Silently they pored over the map.

Then Otto gave an exclamation.

"Do you realise what this map is?" he said. "I think—yes, I'm sure. I know that point. And that. Yes, here's that peak. That's just about the right distance. That cross must represent the cave. Don't you see? It's a map of part of the Blue Glacier. The cave is immediately below the peak, somewhere below the foot of the glacier."

To prove his point, Otto produced his own large-scale map of the district. It tallied in every respect. It was clear that whoever had drawn the map on that sheet of paper had copied it from some such printed map, only omitting all names.

"The whole darned place will be under snow," said Lewis. "How d'you start finding a cave under twelve feet of snow without you dig up the whole mountain?"

Otto's eyes were still fixed on the paper.

"The cross looks to me exactly under that very steep cliff face. Did you notice the one I mean, just this end of the glacier?" he asked.

"I did," said Will. "Looked about a thousand feet sheer. No snow on it."

"That's the one. Look here! This is it, I'm positive."

Otto had turned down the last fold of paper, to disclose a sketch in rough line-work. It showed what seemed to be the base of a wall of cliff, and out of the base stood a stone of a most curious shape. At first it appeared to have no likeness, then a giant's head seemed to look from the rock —a huge misshapen Caliban of a rock. Between the cliff face and the rock, another cross was marked.

Otto looked round, his eyes suddenly blazing with adventure.

"That stone must still be there," he said. "It's

unmistakable. I shall go at once. I must set her mind at rest."

"You don't go without me," said Will firmly.

"Or me," said Rosamund.

This last statement caused much argument. Rosamund was quite unfit for more adventures that night, but with the obstinacy of the very weary refused flatly not to be allowed to share in this great moment.

"It's going to mean climbing," warned Otto. "And some pretty nasty heights. Do be a sensible girl and stay here. You don't know what you're in for."

"I don't care, I'll be all right, honestly I will." Warmed and fed and with the prospect of treasure ahead, Rosamund's will-power had returned if nothing else.

Eventually she had her way and preparations for the expedition were soon in full swing.

"I'll tell Fritz to lock the house up thoroughly behind us," said Otto. "Not that I think there's any fear of our friends turning up to-night from what you say. But it will comfort Fritz and Anna. What about you, Lewis? Are you coming with us?"

Lewis flushed uncomfortably.

"I'd like to," he muttered. "Gee, I'd like to. But I've no head for heights. I just want to pitch straight over. I guess I'd best stay here."

He looked wretched, no doubt aware that he was lowering himself in their eyes. However, no one voiced any opinion. Otto gave hurried instructions to Fritz, who hobbled off to return with a length of rope and a hurricane lantern. In a few minutes the expedition was ready to set off, Rosamund devoutly hoping that her aching limbs would be equal to this new strain.

Otto threw open the front door.

"The moon is perfect for it," he announced. "We've several hours in hand. Rosamund, take this end of the rope. I'll give you a pull. I'm as fresh as a daisy."

Rosamund thankfully assented, and the party, having fitted on their skis, moved forward into the night.

The climb from the chalet to the slopes below the Blauer Gletscher was not great either in height or distance, and excitement seemed to have lent Rosamund new strength. In less than half an hour they stood gazing upwards to the snowfields that hid the glacier from them.

"All right?" Otto asked Rosamund. "Now we begin climbing."

Rosamund nodded, her heart in her boots, for she could see now only too clearly, how high above them lay the jutting black cliffs that formed the buttress for the Blauer Gletscher.

Backwards and forwards they traversed, taking the slope at an easy angle, endlessly, endlessly. The valley, in the silver-blue light, lay thousands of feet below them. Every now and then Otto halted to search the white slopes with his eyes that led to the Blumenthal Pass. There was not a movement, not a sound.

An hour passed. The moon lay farther down in the sky, casting long shadows from each mound.

More and more did Rosamund have to rely on the strength that came from Otto's rope. He seemed tireless.

"Stick to my tracks, Will," he called out. "We start the bad going from here."

"Looks as though the giants had a rugger scrum here," remarked Will, gazing up at the curious rock formations, a succession of vast boulders, rearing like white mammoths out of the snowfield.

"Are we . . . nearly . . . at the glacier?" panted Rosamund.

"Ye gods, no!" laughed Otto. "Luckily we don't need to get there or you'd be climbing for another couple of hours. Distances are very deceptive on a mountain. No, we have only to reach that cliff face up there. Another twenty minutes should do it."

They made their way between the vast white pillars of stone to a further smooth stretch beyond.

Otto called another halt.

"Unpleasant place, that," he remarked. "It's somewhere up above there that the crevasse lies— the one I told you about. Fritz says they call it the Devil's Passage because it has no bottom and leads straight down to Hell. I don't know about Hell, but I do know that it's so deep and narrow that the one or two unwary who have fallen into it have never been recovered. I must make a collection of the local stories one day."

"All round, a pretty jolly spot, this," said Will cheerfully. "If only there were a few bogles and ghosties about, we could make quite a chatty night of it. Why were the people such asses as to go near the crevasse?"

"Pig-headed, and wouldn't take a guide, I suppose," said Otto.

"The place gets covered in snow, but I suppose the current of air keeps it from being more than superficial. Now, from here onwards, we've got to use our heads. That obviously is the cliff face. Look again at the map. Yes, there's that queer sort of arm sticking out. We must aim for the central bit."

"This is no end of a good look-out," said Will, glancing down. "You can get a clear view almost to the Pass. Old Brüne would be visible for a couple of miles if he decided to toddle over to the chalet. We could pretend we were Old Nick and shy some boulders down on him. Almost wish he'd come."

Again the traverse began, up and up and up.

At last they stood right under the dark face of the cliff, so smooth-surfaced, that only a sprinkle of snow clung on ledges here and there.

"Otto, look!" shouted Will.

He had branched from them some yards to the right. He now stood in the shadow of a huge rock.

Otto hastened towards him.

"You're right!" he cried. "We're here!"

Rosamund pressed on to join them. Yes, even though on three sides the snow lay deep upon it, the Epstein giant could be seen, a vast snowman made for no child's pleasure.

"Now what?" demanded Will.   "Do we go round tapping the rock to see if it's hollow? Wish I'd got my knuckle shields.   Let's have another squint at the map.   Surely there's something to go by."

Otto switched on his torch and again they scanned the slip of paper.

"Give me the torch," said Rosamund suddenly. "I've got an idea."

She flashed the light up and down the rocky surface of the cliff.

"There, I told you so!" she cried triumphantly.

The others gave a shout of excitement.   The cross on the map was no mere mark.   For on the rock, above a narrow ledge, sheltered from the snow by a huge overhanging mass of stone, a cross had been scratched.   The boulders were piled there one upon the other, the top boulder all but bare of snow due to the overhang and the arm of rock that half encircled it.   The cross lay above the uppermost boulder.

Otto unfastened his skis.

"Can you give me a leg up?" he asked Will.

With Will's assistance, he managed to find a foothold on one of the lower boulders, sinking only up to the knees in snow.   The second boulder had even less snow on it.   A moment later he was standing on the ledge above their heads.

"Amazing spot this," he called.   "Almost a cave in itself.   Now I wonder.   Stand clear.   I'm going to give this boulder a push."

Rosamund and Will moved to one side.

"Hadn't we better get up first?" cried Will.   "If

you move that boulder, it won't be any too easy."

This certainly seemed sound. Will handed up the hurricane lantern and helped Rosamund on to the first boulder. With Otto's hands leaning over to pull her up, it was simple to reach the ledge. A moment later, and Will had joined them.

The smallest boulder lay on the ledge beside them, directly under the roughly carved cross.

Otto began to push. The boulder was of great weight and its base was wedged under the lower stones. Will leaned over, and attempted to add his weight, a difficult process owing to the narrowness of the ledge.

"Sickening if we can't get it to move," he groaned. "Bet your bottom dollar the opening of the cave is back there. Get on, you brute! Budge, won't you? Gertcher!"

"Let's heave together," said Otto. "Can you reach? Now, one, two, three, go!"

There was a rasping sound of rock on rock, and with a lurch that cast a spray of snow into their faces, the boulder fell with a dull thud among its snow-covered brethren below.

But the three had no eyes for its fate.

All their attention was on the long slit in the rock which now lay open before them.

CHAPTER TEN

JOURNEY'S END

"Otto, I'm frightened!" Rosamund caught frantically at Otto's hand, as he thrust his shoulders into the opening.

Otto turned back to look at her. The moon had turned his fair hair and the gay, handsome face to an ashen silver. For a moment the shocking thought leapt through Rosamund's mind, so would he look if he were dead, so still and so pale.

"Poor Rose!" he said softly. "You're tired out. Only a moment now and we shall be on our way home."

But the kindness in his voice could do nothing to still the sickening terror that filled her at sight of that dark slit in the rock.

Will was on his knees, peering in.

"Shine the torch right in," he said. "Look, there's a sort of a passage. I can just squeeze in. Can you?"

The hurricane lantern in one hand, the torch pointing ahead, Otto pressed himself sideways into the cleft.

"Pretty tight squeeze," he called back. "I'm through now. Good lord, there's quite a big room in here! It's an extraordinary place."

"Don't leave me behind!" begged Rosamund. "Oh, please, I'm so frightened!"

Will patted her.

"You're all in, that's the trouble," he said. "Here, you squeeze through next and I'll follow. That's a good girl. Easy does it. All right?"

Rosamund edged herself through the gap, Will following close behind her. The fissure bent sharply to the left, then opened out.

"Well, well, well!" remarked Will. "Looks as though we're paying a call on Old Nick after all. D'you think this is the office where he keeps his ledgers? Bet he's got old Brüne chalked up for a fireside chair."

Rosamund stood silent, so fascinated by the cave that the quest was almost forgotten.

It was quite a small room, not more than eight feet long and possibly four feet wide. It must have been caused by a settlement in the mountains thousands of years before, for the stratum of the rock was almost vertical. High above them the rock curved, making it impossible to judge the true height of the cave. A great jagged tooth of rock rose from the centre of the cave, joining the rock above to form an archway.

Otto was on his knees in the far corner.

"I've found them," he said. He rose, and carried a brass-studded box over to the lantern. He fitted a key into the lock.

"This key was folded in the map," he murmured. "I hope to heavens it's the right one."

Rosamund and Will watched breathlessly over his shoulder.

The lid rose. There, on a bed of yellowing satin, lay the emerald necklace and bracelet, glowing liquid green stones set with diamonds. Even to Will and Rosamund's unprofessional eyes, they were obviously worth a king's ransom.

Will flashed the torch over them and the stones glittered back at them. Otto picked them up and turned them in his fingers.

"Do you wonder Great-grandmamma didn't want to give them up?" he murmured. "Rosamund, give me your wrist. Let's see what the bracelet looks like."

Rosamund shrank back, her eyes dilated with fear.

"No, no!" she cried. "Otto, shut them up! I don't know what it is—but I feel they don't want to be opened. Do shut them up! Let's go home quickly!"

The two boys looked at her in amazement.

"My dear old thing, pull yourself together!" said Will earnestly. "Not like you to go and get all hysterical. Here, have some of my chocolate."

Otto looked at her strangely. Something of her mood seemed to pass to him.

"Perhaps you're right, Rose," he said. "Perhaps we ought to have left them where they were. I wonder." He looked thoughtfully at the box.

Will shook him by the arm.

"Look here, I'm not going to let Rose's imagination dish you out of a hundred thousand pounds!" he protested. "Be a sensible fellow and let's go home. Shove 'em in your pocket. After all, the Gräfin asked you to get them. You can't disappoint her."

"No, I suppose not." Otto snapped the clasp

of the necklace. "I wonder who found this place? I wonder—— Ah, I know what it is! Fritz told me that near the Devil's Passage there was a place called the Devil's Parlour. The peasants never come this way, but I suppose someone once discovered the place and christened it. Will, you've got the torch. Let's get out of this dreary place. We shall freeze if we stay here much longer. You lead!"

Will walked over to the cleft in the rock. He switched on his torch. A queer sound came from him, a strangled cry that was half a groan. The others stood behind him, their eyes riveted to the spot where the torch lighted the entry. It glinted on to a hand that grasped a revolver, a hand as small and white as a woman's.

CHAPTER ELEVEN

THE DARK HOUR

"WILL you step back please," said a quiet voice, the same voice that Rosamund had heard in the hotel passage. "You will please to put your hands above your heads. The jewels you will put back in the box, Herr von Vierling."

There was nothing for it but to obey.

The revolver and the hand were followed by the body of Herr Brüne, his face was as emotionless as ever. He stood quietly watching the three while another figure entered the cave. It was Signor Mazzini.

No word was spoken. The Italian seized the box and clasped it to him. He knelt down by the hurricane lamp, fingering the jewels, twisting them, turning them to the light, running them through his fingers. His face was working in some sort of ecstasy, the face of a fanatic.

Herr Brüne allowed him a moment or two, then with a quick word of instruction he handed him the revolver. He slipped his hand into his pocket and walked over to the three.

"Please do not move," he said. "If you do, my friend will shoot."

There was menace in the very quietness of the words. This was no romantic villain to gloat over his victims or enjoy his power over them. Here was a man moved by no emotion. The very matter-of-factness with which he treated the situation was inhuman.

"May we ask what you intend to do?" asked Otto steadily.

Brüne raised his expressionless dark eyes.

"I must trouble you to hold out your wrists," he said. "The three of you attached—so—will take a long while to make the journey home. Long enough to allow my friend and I to catch our train."

He had produced from his pocket a long chain of thin steel links. He slipped the end over Otto's wrist and wound it round Rosamund's. There was a click as he snapped a tiny padlock into the links. Drawing the chain over Rosamund's shoulders, he proceeded to secure her other wrist to Will's in the same fashion. The three were, to all intents and purposes, handcuffed tightly together.

Otto's face was white with fury, but with Rosamund between him and the pointed revolver, he could only submit. When he spoke, his voice was as quietly polite as Brüne's.

"If we are not detaining you from your train," he said, "may we ask certain questions that have puzzled us? Will you have the kindness to tell us who you are and how you knew that the jewels were in existence?"

Even the contempt in his voice roused no anger in Brüne's face. He stooped to assure himself that the padlocks were secure, then stepped back from them. He glanced at his wrist-watch.

"If you wish, I will tell you," he said. "I followed you from England. Of the jewels I have known for many years. My father was valet to the Graf von Eldheim. I resemble my father most remarkably, so I am told. The Gräfin noticed the likeness. She had the condescension to mention it. As I had anticipated, she had forgotten that the likeness was not to the features of the Graf von Eldheim, but to my father, whom she knew well. At one time my father was here, in her service. It was when she first came to this country, when the admirable Fritz was on holiday. It seems that the Gräfin told my father of the emeralds and confided to him that she had certain superstitions about these jewels, and that she wished them to be taken and hidden far from the house, where they could no longer bring her ill-luck. My father agreed to hide the box for her. One man, a fellow from the village, had found this cave on one of his rambles. The peasants feared these slopes and the fellow himself swore that he would never again dare approach the cave though he described the position of it to my father. It was perfect as a place of concealment."

"So your father sent you to collect the jewels?" said Otto. "I should hardly have expected him to wait fifty years."

Brüne still showed no anger at the bitter words.

"You misunderstand," he said. "My father, on Fritz's return, went back to the service of von Eldheim, but he was misguided enough to tell no one of the jewels until just before his death.

It was most regrettable, for by then his mind was wandering. He described, during these fits of wandering, over and over again the mountain —the cave—his talks with the Gräfin—the cross over the entrance—everything. But when questioned, he could not recall the name of the mountain, nor even the name of the country, nor the year it took place. That I could roughly judge, but most regrettable of all, he could not tell me the name of the Gräfin. After his death, I made many inquiries. I found that he had once been in the service of the Gräfin von Vierling, but too many years had passed. None knew where the honoured lady had lived. The world is a large place and the task of tracing her was too difficult. Besides, the jewels might long ago have been taken from the cave. Still, I never forgot the story. I have great patience. Many years pass. Then I see in the newspapers your change of name, Herr von Vierling. Chance had come my way and I was grateful. I hired a room by your house. Your address was in the papers, if you remember. I again have to show great patience. Sooner or later he will go to see his great-grandmother, I say. Most inconsiderately, the address of the Gräfin had not also been published in the newspaper. Last week my patience was rewarded."

"Good lord, do you mean to say you sat and watched out of the window for two months and more?" Will's interest in the story had almost made him forget their situation.

"Naturally not." There was nothing that savoured of gloating in Brüne's explanation. He spoke as any craftsman might of a job well accomplished. "No, no. I became acquainted with the young woman who works daily for your mother. I tell her I am a reporter. I tell her she will receive five pounds and her photograph in all the papers if she will inform me when Mr. Otto contemplates going abroad. Young women will do most things to see their photograph in the newspapers."

"And may I ask why you made those attempts on my life?" asked Otto. "How would my death help you find the jewels?"

Brüne shrugged his shoulders.

"It was a precaution," he admitted. "After our first interview with the Gräfin we knew that the jewels were still hidden in the mountains. So much she told us. As the son of an old friend, I took the liberty of asking if she were in any need of financial aid. She assured me not, and that her heir would be wealthy as she had jewels of fabulous wealth hidden away. My friend Mazzini was in great excitement, for those jewels are mentioned in history. They disappeared from the family of the Grand Duke and many collectors have tried to discover them. Mazzini was in great fear also that we could not keep sufficient watch upon your movements. You might be sent to fetch the emeralds before we could locate the cave. I saw his point. I did not wish to disappoint Signor Mazzini. He is my very good client."

Rosamund could feel Otto's clenched fingers

against her hand, though when he spoke again his voice was as quiet as before.

"You had better tell us the whole story, Brüne," he said. "It's unlikely that we shall meet again. There is a great deal more that I want to know."

Rosamund glanced up at him in bewilderment. It seemed to her, in her fright and weariness, a little selfish and stupid of him, just to go on letting Brüne talk to satisfy his curiosity, when she would give all that she had to be struggling back to the warmth and safety of the chalet. It was almost as though Otto wanted to prolong this dreadful scene.

Brüne glanced again at his watch.

"What is it that you wish to know? There is little time. We have to catch a train in Interbuhl. Yes, Herr von Vierling, I changed the screws on your skis. It was simple, for they stood in the stand next to mine. It was an experiment but not a successful one. Ah yes, the flags. That was even more simple. Since leaving the Grand, I have lived at the Belle Vue in the valley. Two English gentlemen with loud voices lunched there and spoke constantly of the course and the fact that Herr von Vierling would try it that afternoon. While they finished their meal, I went to the course. They had spoken of the flags placed at a sufficient distance from the rocks. To move the flags was very simple for no one was about. But Mr. Vierling's skill avoided the sad catastrophe. Then we did not know until later, for I had promised my friend Mazzini to meet him that afternoon at the chalet to try once more to find out from the Gräfin if there was a map of the mountains and the cave in her possession. Unluckily my friend was a little impetuous. At the time we thought the honourable lady was past recovery. We could not wait to search the room owing to the interference of the servants."

There was a snort from Will at this admirable piece of under-statement.

"Do let them go!" murmured Rosamund.

But Otto seemed not to hear her.

"You haven't explained yet about the priest's disguise," he demanded.

Brüne gave a little deprecating shrug of his shoulders.

"That was not as it should be," he admitted. "My friend Mazzini had the foolishness to place the wig behind the drawer and the far greater foolishness of forgetting to tell me it was there. When we discovered the loss, it was necessary for me to return to the hotel and to ask to make search. As I was about to enter the hotel, I noticed that the window of my former room was open. I took the chance, for I was not anxious to make my return known. But the time was insufficient and I had to retire. I watched Miss Burnaby leaning from the window. It was foolish of her to interfere in my business. I booked a room in the hotel and asked permission to search for some missing letters. As I thought, the package was gone. It was returned to me later, but I was fully convinced that Miss Burnaby had opened it. I had to change my plans. It had been

my intention to go to the chalet early in the
morning disguised as a priest, in the hope of
either receiving the Gräfin's confidence or being
able to search her room for the map which I was
so sure must be in her possession. Mazzini had
already installed himself in the hayloft at the
chalet so that he might follow Herr von Vierling's
movements. I decided to set out immediately,
for Miss Burnaby will certainly tell Herr von
Vierling in the morning."

"So you weren't following us! You were
ahead!" The words seemed almost jerked out of
Rosamund.

"That is so, Miss. Our plans once more have
to change, for as Mazzini and I discuss at what
hour of morning or possibly night a priest might
call upon a dying lady, we hear sounds, and Miss
Burnaby and the American gentleman arrive. I
again trust to chance. We see three again set
out. Surely it must be to find the jewels. We
follow. We are saved the trouble of the long and
difficult search for the cave for you lead us to it.
It is good business to allow others to save one
time and trouble. Yes, there have been errors,
but on the whole it has been well done. The
Signor Mazzini is my good client. He loves
precious stones as if they were his little children.
He will pay much money for them."

All this while, Mazzini had squatted by the
lantern, one hand clasping the revolver, the other
grasping the jewels, the sallow, vulture-like head
peering from one to another of their faces. Now,
at a sudden order from Brüne, he lurched to his

feet and came towards them, his revolver pointing full at Rosamund.

Rosamund glanced up at Otto for comfort, but his face had grown so pale that her own fears were redoubled. She turned to Will. She saw his eyes were fixed on Brüne.

"I don't get this." It was Will speaking. "Why have you been telling us all this? Aren't you frightened we'll tell the police?"

"No, Mr. Burnaby."

Brüne was glancing again at his watch. He spoke again to Mazzini in rapid Italian.

With the revolver still pointing at Rosamund, Mazzini caught Will by the shoulder and jerked him two or three feet forward.

"Your other wrist if you please, Mr. Burnaby," said Brüne. "Do not resist me, Herr von Vierling, otherwise my friend Mazzini will be obliged to shoot the young lady."

"You can't do it!" breathed Otto. "You will be brought to justice for it! You will be condemned to death and the jewels will be useless to you. I am prepared to bargain. Let us leave here immediately and I will give my word of honour to make no statement to the police."

Still the meaning of Brüne's actions was not clear to Rosamund. The sight of that revolver pointing at her, the dark, hollow-eyed face of the Italian so near to her, watching her intently, yet with no thought of her but as a thread in the weaving of his plans, filled her with such a sense of unreality and dread that her wits were blunted.

"Otto, Otto, what are they going to do

with us?" Will's voice came to her, sharp in its fear. She noticed that another chain now bound Will's wrist to Otto's. They formed a circle, fastened tightly to each other, wrist to wrist, and in the centre of the circle was the stone pillar that arched to the roof.

So that was why Brüne had told them all that they had asked! He had never intended that they should leave the cave.

A faint gasping sob came from Will, but Rosamund was silent. Her exhaustion stood her in good stead. Her poor weary mind could scarcely grasp the new horror that had come to them.

Mazzini had gathered the jewels into his breast pocket. The box lay still on the floor. Rosamund found herself gazing at the once-white satin, at the little dints that marked the place where the emeralds had lain.

She heard Will pleading in English, pathetically, his courage for the moment broken by the thought of what lay before them.

"It's no good," Otto said huskily. "They're going through with it. Oh, what a fool I was to bring you here!"

Rosamund watched Mazzini pick up the hurricane lantern and edge himself through the entrance. Brüne made to follow him.

"I am very sorry this should have to happen," he said. "Believe me, very sorry. But in business one cannot afford to have sentiment."

"You'll hang for this!" shouted Will.

"I think not." Brüne weighed his words. "No,

I think not. It is now snowing a little, enough to cover all tracks. No one knows of the cave. The cold here is great. Even if members of your household know that you set out on this errand, it will take them many, many hours to find you. I do not frankly think you will be alive by then. So, you see, it is good business."

There was something indescribably callous about the man's attitude. It was clear that the death of three human beings moved him not at all, if their lives in any way interfered with his business.

His slight body passed with ease between the rocks. There was a noise beyond, of boots scraping on stone, and then silence, a silence so complete that it filled the cave with that dead weight of silence that can be more overpowering than sound. Only Otto's torch lay on the ground, a fading glimmer of light.

A little groan escaped from Otto. "What am I to say?" he muttered. "Ghastly, idiotic, blundering fool that I've been. To have mixed you both up in this, risked your lives and now . . . Why didn't I tell Fritz where we were going?"

"Lewis saw the map," said Will. "When we don't come home, he'll get up a search-party. Gosh, I'm cold."

"He won't know what time to expect us back," said Otto grimly. "Look! We've got to face up to this. There is no chance of any rescue party till the morning. We've got to keep moving. The cold in here is going to be our worst trouble. Can you get your other hand round to my wrist,

Will, and see if the chain is impossible to slip off?"

There was silence, while Will attempted to draw his two wrists together. The stone pillar cut into their hands, but it was useless. The distance was too great.

Suddenly Rosamund slipped to the floor.

"I'm so . . . tired," she murmured. "I must go to sleep. Oh, Otto, you're hurting my wrist!"

Sharply Otto had jerked her to her feet. She began to cry in her weakness and pain.

"Rose darling, listen." Otto's voice rang in her ears. "We've got to keep going. We've got to fight against this cold. It will begin to have a very bad effect on us if we stay still. We must walk round and round. Do try, my dear! Try hard."

Slowly they circled round the pillar, a grim ring-o'-roses played in the ice-cold of the cave. Every few steps Rosamund stumbled, but always she was pulled again to her feet by the pain in her wrists. Her little moans were the only sound as the minutes passed by. Otto's torch had grown dim. It flickered, and the light was gone. Only a thin streak of grey showed through the entrance.

"Would it be any good shouting?" asked Will brokenly.

"I don't think so, but we can try. Rosamund, you shout too. It'll help to keep you warm."

They shouted again and again, the sound echoing up the walls above them. No hope lay behind those voices.

"How . . . long . . . can we . . . stand this?" Will's lips were stiff with cold.

"I don't know." Otto's voice came from the darkness. "I . . . really don't know. If only we could get at Rosamund. We're hurting her so. But we must keep going, must keep going."

The everlasting circling began again, round and round in that black emptiness, while the jagged stone of the pillar caught at their clothes and at their outstretched arms. The stumbles grew more frequent, and after one fall, not even the pain in her wrists could rouse Rosamund.

The end was coming nearer.

"There is nothing more we can do now," said Otto slowly. "We can go on shouting if you like. It will . . . do no harm."

They shouted again, a curious sound it was, from between those numbed lips.

"Anyway . . . we raised . . . a good echo," gasped Will. "Unless . . ."

"Yes! I heard it too!" There was a sudden breathless hope in Otto's voice. "Shout again!"

The thin sound rose once more.

"There!"

An answering shout had come from below. It was no echo. It was a definite shout of "Hallo there!"

"Good lord, it's Lewis!" Will strained frantically towards the grey patch of light. "Lewis! Lewis!"

The answer came back almost immediately.

"Hold hard there, you fellows!"

There was the sound of clambering feet against the ledge. A moment later, a torch shone into the cave, and following the torch, the anxious face of Lewis.

It was no moment for explanations or heroics. Scarcely a word was spoken. Lewis had sized up the situation instantly. Among the gadgets that bristled from his pocket-knife, was a small hacksaw blade. The torch between his teeth, he set to work on the thin steel rings. It was only a few moments before first Otto and then Will were freed.

Otto bent over Rosamund to lift her in his arms. She was quite unconscious.

"There's brandy in my pocket," he said. "Pour some out. My hands are numb."

Lewis obeyed, and Otto tried to force a few drops between Rosamund's lips.

"We've got to get home quickly," he muttered. "Will, drink some of this. You too, Lewis."

The brandy flask was passed between them.

They made their way through the entrance, carrying Rosamund with difficulty between them through that narrow slit.

The moon had sunk almost to the horizon of the far mountains. There were heavy clouds overhead, but the faint flurry of snow was over. The light seemed dazzling to their eyes after the darkness.

"Did you see Brüne? Which way did he go?" asked Will.

"Up there." Lewis pointed above them to the right. "I had to wait till they were out of sight. Afraid they'd put back and put me in the bag too if they saw me."

"Up where, did you say?" Otto stared upwards. "Good lord! Do you imagine they're trying to take the short way over to Interbuhl? They can't do it from here unless they cross the glacier."

His keen eyes swept the heights above.

"Look!" The boys followed his eyes. Far, far above them, were two tiny black figures, making for the white pass east of the Teufelspitz, even now crossing the great snowfield that hid the Blauer Gletscher.

"Will they make it?" asked Will.

"Possibly. The snow is quite heavy. Keep in the shadow, both of you. They mustn't see us."

Otto glanced down to the limp burden in his arms.

"Otto, look!" gasped Will. "Something's happening!"

For on the stillness of the night had come a cry, a cry of mortal fear. Only one black figure was now on the mountainside. It seemed to sway for an instant, then another cry was borne faintly on the air, a sound that is only uttered once, once at the moment before death. There was silence. The snowfield lay empty in the moonlight.

"What . . . what's happened?" whispered Lewis.

Otto turned away.

"Get down and help me on with my skis," he commanded briefly. "We can go now."

"But what's happened?" cried Will.

Otto's face was grim.

"The Devil's Passage," he said. "It's Brüne and Mazzini who will never be found alive."

CHAPTER TWELVE

FAREWELL TO REINIGEN

ROSAMUND lay in bed, looking up at the white ceiling. Her eyes travelled round the green line that divided it from the cream of the wall. She followed it down the curve of the window.

There her eyes paused and stared at an unexpected sight.

Miss Drover sat by the window in an easy-chair, book in hand. She glanced round and met Rosamund's bewildered gaze. She came over to the bed.

"Feeling better, m'dear?" she said. "Nice fright you gave us all."

"I . . . I . . ." Rosamund stammered. Then, in a sickening flash, the memory of the night came to her. "How . . . But the cave? We were in the cave . . . I was so tired . . ."

"All right, dear, all right. Every one is quite safe. Drink some of this and have a little food. Dr. Sawday was very anxious for you to eat when you woke."

Rosamund was still quite bewildered.

"How did I get here?" she cried. "Oh dear, I'm so stiff! And my wrists . . . they're bandaged."

"I know." Miss Drover's loud voice was very gentle. "You had a very terrible experience. Otto told me all about it. Nothing to worry about now. Will's none the worse, nor Lewis."

"And Otto?"

"Otto is over at the chalet. Hopes to get back to see you soon. Very worried about you, poor fellow. D'you realise he carried you all the way here over his shoulder? At great speed too. He thought you were almost frozen. They sent out a rescue party for Will and Lewis. Poor lads, they'd only made the head of the Blumenthal. They were all in. Fit as fleas now, though. Wish you could have seen the breakfast they ate. Lewis busy cooking up a tale to tell Mrs. V. that won't give her palpitations. Can't keep it dark. Hardly move for stiffness, either of them."

"Lewis! Then was it Lewis who rescued us?" Rosamund's eyes filled with pleasure.

"Gathered so. Not going to spoil his story though. He'll tell you himself. Just let Sawday have a peep at you first. Sat up two hours with you, he did. Decent chap. Don't dare to get up while I'm gone!"

Rosamund laughed weakly. "I don't think I could if I tried," she said. "Do please let me see the others. There's so much I want to know."

Dr. Sawday was entirely satisfied with his patient.

"What a thing it is to be young," he remarked to Miss Drover. "Stay in bed to-morrow, young lady, and we'll have you dancing at the fancy-dress ball by Saturday. Visitors? Of course. Let her see who she likes."

A few moments later Miss Drover had returned with Will and Lewis, slightly heavy-eyed, but otherwise looking none the worse.

"You'd better tell her everything," advised Miss Drover. "It won't hurt her."

Will nodded. He passed swiftly over those moments of horror after she had lost consciousness, dwelling only on the wonderful moment when Lewis's answering shout had come to them. He told her of the fate of Brüne and Mazzini.

"What will happen about them? Have the police been called?" asked Rosamund.

"Herr Geitzler has been looking after all that," said Lewis. "A party went out this morning to see if it was possible to rescue the bodies, but the tracks showed that they went in at just about the worst spot. No, Mazzini and Brüne are there for keeps—and the emeralds. Lucky thing Otto seems so calm about losing them. Won't even tell any one that Mazzini had them on him. I believe he's quite glad they're gone. Jolly catching, superstitions."

Rosamund shivered.

"The police are being very decent," continued Will. "Otto refused to make a charge against the men, just reported that he saw two chaps disappear into the crevasse. The porter confirmed he'd seen Brüne leaving the hotel late last night, and there were the tracks to prove it. Wonder what they made of the empty jewel-case in the cave. They must have followed the tracks down there. Seems Mazzini has a very decent Swiss wife. Otto's keen she shouldn't find out what Mazzini was up to, that's why it's all being hushed up. Jolly nice of him, what?"

"But, Lewis, how did you know what was happening?" cried Rosamund.

"Easy," said Lewis. "I was sitting there kicking myself for not having gone with you. I thought I'd take another peek through the hall window to see if you were still in sight, and what did I see but that blighter Mazzini making off up the drive. I could see Brüne too. He'd started off up the path after you. Old Fritz came in and I tried to tell him about it, but we didn't get along so hot. So I just lighted out after 'em. I daren't let 'em get too far ahead and I daren't stick too tight on their heels for fear they'd look round. Still it wasn't too hard. There were plenty of bends on that route."

"Lewis, how terribly brave of you!" Rosamund's eyes shone.

"Don't you believe it. I was scared stiff. Well, on we went. Never got a glimpse of you folk. My chaps must have branched off a bit and done their climbing earlier. Climbing! It was like following them up the side of a house. I'd never have kept up only Mazzini didn't seem any great shakes on skis either. They kept stopping for a breather. Several times I saw them point. You people must just have been in sight. The last bit was the worst. It was beginning to snow too. There wasn't any cover but I dodged down behind a boulder and watched them climb on to the ledge and disappear. Thought you might be in there too, but daren't investigate or they'd have put me in the bag too. Boy, was it cold waiting for them to come out! Couldn't have stood it much longer, wondering what they were doing to you. I couldn't hear a sound, so I still had half a hope you'd been taking it easy and I'd see you coming up the slope before long."

"But why did we never see them if they could see us?" asked Rosamund.

"They were right above you all the time," explained Lewis. "Well, after they'd come out, I had to wait a great while before they'd got up and away. They were going very slow. Still no signs of you people, so I thought I'd better take a look round. Then I heard your first shout. I suppose you couldn't hear me answer from that way off. I daren't yell out too loud as Brüne and Mazzini weren't all that way off. Took me ages to get up to you. I'd got pretty stiff waiting around. Then I heard the shout again. That's all."

"Fine bit of work, Lewis," commented Miss Drover. "Don't you know it's those who get scared but carry on that are the really brave?"

Lewis flushed with pleasure and Will patted his shoulder.

"He's the best of fellows," he said warmly, and Lewis smiled back at him.

"What did you do after that—that awful thing happened to the others?" pursued Rosamund.

"That wasn't so funny for Will and me," grinned Lewis. "Old Otto must be as tough as nails. He got us all fixed on our skis and told us to make for the hotel. There wasn't much in it in distance and he wanted to get a doctor to you. He slings you over his shoulder as though you were two pints worth of nothing, and off we go."

"Lewis and I just couldn't hold up," went on Will. "We tobogganed most of the way down when we weren't playing bumps-a-daisy with the boulders. When we were on the track, Otto said he must get on quickly on his own. We had a go at getting back, but by George, we weren't half pleased when some chaps came along and raked us in. I suppose you know Miss Drover's been sitting up with you since about four o'clock this morning?"

"I didn't!" cried Rosamund penitently. "How very sweet of you. I'm sorry to have been such a nuisance."

"You haven't. Enjoyed it," declared Miss Drover. "Couldn't sleep anyway. Thought you were up to something last night. Worried about you. Well, all over now. Quite agree with Otto. Tell no one. Least said soonest mended."

At that moment there was a knock at the door.

It was Otto who stood in the doorway, his eyes fixed anxiously on Rosamund.

"Come in!" called Miss Drover. "Excellent night. Looks as though you could do with some sleep yourself. Nothing to worry about here. Had any food to-day? Thought not. How's the Gräfin?"

Otto closed the door.

"She died this morning," he said quietly. "Very peacefully. The doctor was there and the priest from Musson. She seemed to know us all just before the end."

"I hope you didn't have to tell her about the

jewels," said Will. "She'd have been so disappointed."

"No," said Otto. "She seemed quite at ease in her mind. Oddly enough, Anna said that a very great change came over her about two o'clock this morning. Until then, she had been very restless. It was at about two o'clock that—those two reached the Devil's Passage."

"There are stranger things in heaven and earth . . ." quoted Miss Drover.

There was a silence.

"One other strange thing happened," said Otto slowly. "Just at the last, she sat up in bed and stretched out her arms. She said quite clearly —in German, of course—' Otto, I knew you would understand.' She wasn't speaking to me. She died immediately afterwards."

Rosamund's eyes filled with tears.

"I don't think any of us will ever forget her," she said. "You were right when you said she was a very great lady."

Letter from Mr. William Burnaby to Mrs. Burnaby, 5 Beck Street, Hampstead, N.W.3

Grand Hotel,
Reinigen. *Jan.* 13*th*

DEAR MUM AND DAD,

How are you? This is to say Rose and I will be hopping on the train the day after to-morrow and will be yours to command by about five on Thursday evening. Do you think you could murmur treacle tart into the Elkin ear for supper

that night? Rose isn't writing. She's hurt her
wrists. She'll be O.K. in a day or two. I played
ice-hockey to-day.   Jolly good fun crashing
around at top speed.   Can't think of any other
news.   Latin Grammar and Geometry in five
days! Bah and also Pfui.

Your loving son,
WILL.

Dud-dud-dud-dud.   Dud-dud-dud-dud.   Dud-
dud-dud-dud.

Green fields, mile upon mile of hedgeless
rolling plains, long, poplar-fringed roads, small
stone farms tucked into hollows, broad placid
rivers—the French countryside passed steadily by
in the light of the early morning.

Curled in a corner of the railway carriage sat
Rosamond, her grey eyes full of thought. Will
sat opposite to her, deep in a magazine.

She patted his knee.

"Will, can you believe it's only fifteen days
since we left England?" she demanded.

" 'Course it is. Count it up and see," said Will's
voice from behind the paper.

Fifteen days.   Men were passing by, shaving
tackle in hand, a patient queue was again gathered
outside the toilettes. Everything was the same as
on the journey out. That evening they would be
sitting round the drawing-room fire, with Mother
in her low chair listening to their stories and
Daddy looking over the *Spectator* to throw in a
remark now and then.   Mrs. Fez-Fusby might

condescend to sit on her knee. Mrs. Elkin would
still be going to bed with the poker for fear of
burglars. Everything would be the same—and
yet, so different. There was so much that could
never be described, so much that might mercifully
be forgotten. She must never think of that night.
It should not be hard, with so much happiness
to dwell on.

She relived again in her mind the few moments
at the station. It had been a great send-off. The
Vandermeyers and Miss Drover and Herr Schlacht
had all come with them to the station. Mrs.
Vandermeyer had shed tears over their departure
and consoled herself by buying the largest possible
box of " candies " for the journey. She had
been kindness itself during those last four days.
A most simple heart lived under all the expensive
clothes, and she and Rosamund had talked long
and earnestly about " managing " Lewis, and
all Rosamund's gentle hints had been accepted
with great humility. Her pleasure in Will and
Lewis's growing friendship had been delightful
to see, and she had warmly accepted Will's invitation for Lewis to spend the Easter holidays at
Hampstead. It was with real respect and affection
that Rosamund had kissed her good-bye and
thanked her again and again for their holiday.

Then Otto had arrived.

She had seen nothing of him during those last
days, for he had flown to Denmark to arrange
for the Gräfin to be buried in the churchyard
where his great-grandfather lay.

They stood on the platform, a little way away

from the laughing voices of the others, while he explained that he had returned to the chalet only the night before.

"Good-bye, Otto." Her words sounded flat and empty. There was an obstinate lump in her throat.

"Dear little Rose!" He had looked down at her with his sweet smile. "A lot more water may have to flow under the bridge before we meet again, and now we've only this moment to say good-bye in. Look. I've got something here for you. Great-grandmamma asked me to give it to you. I told you that she was quite clear in her mind and knew us all just before the end. Open it."

He had handed her a small leather case. In it lay the Gräfin's diamond cross.

"Oh, Otto," murmured Rosamund. "I can't take anything so beautiful! She can't have meant it for me!"

People were climbing into the funicular. There was a warning shout from the guard.

"Please keep it for the present," said Otto hurriedly. "You may want to give it back later. I shall come and ask you what you feel about it in a year or two. You see, she attached a condition to it. I'm very much afraid—if you want to keep the cross—you have to keep me."

"Rose, for Pete's sake, come on!" shouted Will. "The bally funicular's going."

"Rose, do you think that condition—will make you want to give it back?"

The blue eyes were very close to the grey.

"I think . . . I'm sure I shall want to keep it," Rosamund had said, and all her loving heart was in the words.

The funicular had started. She had waved her handkerchief to the little group on the platform. It was finished. No, only part of it was finished. Somewhere in the future, a golden world would be hers for ever.

The fields of France had given way to the sand-dunes of the coast.

Rosamund leaned forward, the little leather case clasped in her hands.

"Hasn't it all been wonderful, Willie?" she said. Will nodded.

THE END